Dear Reader,

When the idea for *The Soldier's Homecoming* came to me, the heroine arrived first. And then a hero showed up, a hero so complicated I loved him already. I had a picture in my mind of what he looked like—I always cast my characters—and I knew what he'd suffered.

I waited a long time to write this story, and when the time came, I knew I had to do it right. Not only for my hero, but for the real men and women who do the difficult jobs so that we don't have to. I researched post-traumatic stress disorder, and with the help of fellow Harlequin Romance® author Nicola Marsh, I got the physiotherapy information I needed. Thanks, Nic!

Then I put out a call for information about the Canadian Armed Forces. Before the day was out, I "met" Doug and Jane Eaton. They put up with e-mail upon e-mail and answered all my questions on the military and special forces eagerly and completely. Thank you, Doug and Jane, for being so generous with your experiences and knowledge. I couldn't have written this without you.

And finally, unbelievable gratitude to my editor, Maddie Rowe, who took this very rough story and helped me turn it into what I envisioned all along—a book about healing, forgiveness and love. Thank you, Maddie, for your incredible enthusiasm, advice and support.

I'm truly blessed.

*Donna*

Because every woman deserves her own
fairy tale, Harlequin Romance® brings you

## Donna Alward

Warmly emotional, enchantingly fresh, this
young Canadian author delivers compelling
stories that will brighten your day!

Previous stories by Donna

*HIRED BY THE COWBOY*
*MARRIAGE AT CIRCLE M*

Don't miss Donna's next story:
*Falling for Mr. Dark & Dangerous*
out in August!

# DONNA ALWARD

*The Soldier's Homecoming*

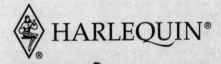

TORONTO • NEW YORK • LONDON
AMSTERDAM • PARIS • SYDNEY • HAMBURG
STOCKHOLM • ATHENS • TOKYO • MILAN • MADRID
PRAGUE • WARSAW • BUDAPEST • AUCKLAND

ISBN-13: 978-0-373-17504-8
ISBN-10:    0-373-17504-3

THE SOLDIER'S HOMECOMING

First North American Publication 2008.

Copyright © 2008 by Donna Alward.

**Printed in U.S.A.**

**Donna Alward** can't remember a time when she didn't love books. When her mother would take her to town, her "treat" wasn't clothes or candy but a trip to the bookstore. This continued through university, where she studied English literature, writing short stories and poetry but never attempting full-length fiction.

In 2001 her sister told her to just get out there and do it, and after completing her first manuscript she was hooked. She lives in Alberta, Canada, with her husband and children, and when not writing is involved in music and volunteering at her children's school.

To find out more about Donna, visit her Web page at www.donnaalward.com or her blog at www.donnaalward.blogspot.com, and sign up for her newsletter!

This book is dedicated to the men and women of our Armed Forces and their families—who put their lives on the line for our freedom every day.

We can never thank you enough.

# CHAPTER ONE

SHANNYN SMITH heard the door open but didn't dare tear her eyes from the column she was adjusting. "Good morning," she said to the figure she knew was in front of the reception counter. There was a glimpse of muted green in her peripheral vision as she input the last series of numbers. "I'll be right with you."

She turned in her office chair, put a stack of patient files on the desk and clicked the mouse, minimizing the table and bringing up today's appointment schedule. Of all days for their receptionist to call in sick, forcing her to fill in. She had monthly reports due. "And you are?"

When no one answered, she lifted her eyes. And the world started to spin dangerously. Dark hair. Green eyes. The khaki color of army combats.

Jonas.

"Sgt. Kirkpatrick to see Ms. Malloy," he answered brusquely. But she knew he recognized her too when his Adam's apple bobbed up, then down as he swallowed hard.

"Jonas," she whispered. That was all. She couldn't bring herself to say more, not with him standing in front of her as if he'd materialized from a dream.

Six long years. Six years since he'd said goodbye to her. Six years since he'd been transferred to Edmonton, leaving her behind here, in Fredericton, New Brunswick, and never looking back.

"Hello, Shannyn."

His words were cold and impersonal. Shannyn knew she couldn't expect anything different, nor did she want to. It had been so long since they'd seen each other. He'd moved on. Perhaps even married. Just because the shock of seeing him made *her* heart give a little flutter, didn't mean it did the same for him. And simply seeing him now suddenly complicated *everything*.

A counter separated them, which was a good thing, Shannyn realized. On the heels of her shock came an irrational spurt of pure joy in knowing he was alive. Despite how things had ended, she'd wondered at times where he was, or if he'd been killed or wounded. The elation of seeing him in the flesh shot through her veins. Yes, it was good that the reception counter was there. If not, she'd have been tempted to jump up and give him an impetuous hug of relief. That would be vastly inappropriate. They were old lovers, a flash from the past. And that was all they would remain. She'd worked too hard to build her life after he'd moved on, so she remained firmly in her seat. He certainly hadn't cared enough to keep in touch, had he? Not a single letter or phone call. Right now it shouldn't matter in the least that he was standing in front of her.

Except it did.

"You look well," she managed, trying a professional smile that fell a little flat as it encountered his stern expression.

He looked amazing, in fact. His hair was military short, but still thick and sable colored. His eyes were large, a beautiful shade of moss green with thick black lashes. When they'd met, it had been his eyes that had been the clincher. It had been his eyes that had stayed with her all this time, making it impossible for her to forget completely.

His tall, firm body was dressed in everyday combats, nothing special, even though he was neat as a pin. She noticed the three stripes on his sleeve. When he'd gone back to Edmonton, Alberta, he'd been a private with his eyes set on being an elite soldier. The best of the best. Obviously his career had progressed. Time had passed.

"Is Ms. Malloy running behind?"

Her weak smile faded and she recoiled. That was all? She hadn't expected old-home week or anything, and didn't want it, either, but pleasantries would have been appropriate under the circumstances. Some acknowledgment that he remembered her.

Clearing her throat, she looked up at the screen. "About ten minutes, that's all. You can have a seat in the waiting room."

He turned from the counter without a word, walked toward the blue padded chairs, and Shannyn stared, her stomach tumbling.

He was limping.

A million thoughts flooded her brain all at once. The overriding one was that he'd been injured, and momentarily all her resentment at his nonexistent reception evaporated. Somehow, somewhere he'd taken "fire and blood", and *his* blood had been spilled. In that split second she imagined it leaking out of his body and soaking into the dry desert earth. Where had he been? In the Middle East, like so many of the Canadian troops? It seemed all they heard of nowadays were the small skirmishes that had devastating results.

On automatic pilot she let Geneva Molloy know that her next appointment had arrived. And what was he doing back here? The last she'd heard, he'd been stationed in Edmonton with his battalion of the Princess Pats. So why was he back at Base Gagetown, after all this time?

She stared at the back of his head, her earlier work forgotten.

She could hardly go up and ask him about it, could she? He'd already been cold and dismissive. Hardly inspiring a heart-to-heart between them.

She discovered it was a conversation she didn't want to have. After years of wondering what it would be like to see him again, to tell him the truth…it was surprising to discover it was not what she wanted. Uppermost in her mind was simply the preservation of the life she'd built for herself.

She'd done what she had for good reasons. To forget that, to be tempted to engage with him, would mean everything would change. The shock of seeing him face-to-face made that abundantly clear. Everything she'd done in the past six years—her silence, her going to night school, running this office—it had been for the best of reasons. She owed nothing to the cold stranger who had suddenly appeared today. Injured or not. He was the one who'd left her behind. He was the one who had decided his career was more important than what they had together.

"Shannyn. You okay?" Carrie Morehouse, one of the therapists, put a hand on Shannyn's shoulder. "You're in another world."

"I'm so sorry." Shannyn straightened and exhaled. "What do you need, Carrie?"

"Mrs. Gilmore's file. Are you sure you're okay? You look like you've seen a ghost."

At that moment Geneva Malloy's voice came through the far door. "Sgt. Kirkpatrick? I'm ready for you now."

Jonas stood, and without a backward glance at Shannyn's desk, went through the door with his physiotherapist.

"Hey…'Kirkpatrick'." Carrie paused, then pierced Shannyn with a questioning look. "Isn't Kirkpatrick the name of—"

Shannyn confirmed it with a twitch of her eyebrow.

Carrie grabbed a nearby chair and pulled it close, plopping down. "Then it is a ghost."

"He's very real, I'm afraid." Shannyn took Mrs. Gilmore's file and handed it over, torn between wanting to talk about it and wanting to pretend he wasn't back at all.

"Did he even recognize you?" The file went forgotten in Carrie's hand.

Maybe it would have been easier if he hadn't recognized her, although after all they'd shared there was little chance of it. It might have been easier to take, though, than the cold reception she'd been given.

"Oh, he knows who I am. He just doesn't seem to care. Which is just as it should be." She tried hard to be glad Jonas had been so cold. If he wasn't interested in her now, it made her life a whole lot easier.

Carrie looked at her watch. "I wish we could talk. I've got to run or I'll be behind. We'll chat later, okay?" Carrie reached over and gave Shannyn's hand a reassuring squeeze.

There was nothing for them to talk about, not really. Jonas would move along soon enough, and she'd still be left behind. After his impersonal greeting this morning, it was very clear he didn't hold any lingering feelings for her at all. That was for the best. Dreams were well and good, but reality was a whole other ball game. She'd learned that the hard way a long time ago. Everything would be much easier this way in the end.

Shannyn sighed. Anything with Jonas would be temporary, no matter how much she'd never been able to completely let go, no matter how tempted she was to go there again. But temporary wasn't good enough. Not anymore.

Shannyn attempted to go back to her monthly reports but her heart wasn't in her work. She kept picturing Jonas's limp and wondered what he was going through with his therapy. Wondered what had brought him to this point in his life.

Questions she had no right to ask.

After an hour had passed, Jonas reappeared at her desk. She looked up at him over the counter. Goodness, he was tall. It was one of the things she'd always really liked about him. Jonas was easily six-one, and seemed to stand even taller after his physio session.

"I need to book my next appointment."

"How frequently are you supposed to have sessions?" Shannyn tried to keep her voice professional and light.

"Once a week, for now."

She opened up the schedule. This was ridiculous. They were talking over appointments as if they were complete strangers. Yet she'd tried already to bridge the gap, make it personal, and he'd been cool and dismissive. She straightened her shoulders. "Next Thursday, two-thirty in the afternoon is all I've got."

"That's fine."

She wrote it on a card for him and started to hand it over the gray counter. But when his fingers closed on it, she knew she couldn't let him go without asking one question.

"Jonas…your leg. It's all right?"

"My leg's fine."

"How long are you on base, then?" Her heart stopped as she finished her second question, unable to help herself.

For a moment, just the space of a breath, his eyes spoke to her, delving in, acknowledging that he wasn't as cold as he seemed. But then he shuttered them. Shannyn knew she hadn't imagined the look. There was still a connection. Perhaps only the memory of what had been, but it was there, and she wished it wasn't. Her life would be much easier if she felt nothing at all.

"This is my station. I have no plans to be going elsewhere in the foreseeable future."

Here, for good? She swallowed. A short visit would have been better. Certainly less risky. But she also knew that "for good" was a relative term. No one in the military was ever in one place for long.

"All right, then," she replied dumbly.

He turned crisply and went to the door, his limp slightly less pronounced than it had been before his appointment.

He left without looking back.

He was really good at that. And she'd do well to remember it.

Shannyn left work on Friday and stopped for pizza. Every payday she stopped for a takeout meal, a biweekly extravagance. Last payday it had been chicken strips and fries. Tonight was Hawaiian pizza, with extra cheese.

She was leaning against the takeout counter when a door slammed just outside and she saw Jonas getting out of a battered four-by-four truck.

What were the chances?

Obviously pretty good. She took a deep breath and turned her attention to the teen behind the counter who was getting her change. As the glass door opened, she tucked the money in her wallet and slid to the side to wait for her order.

"Pickup for Kirkpatrick," he said to the girl in the red-and-white visor.

He dug out his wallet and turned with the box in his hands, stopping short when he saw her waiting to the side.

"Shannyn."

"Small world, huh?" She attempted a faint but cool smile.

"Bachelor's supper," he replied civilly, lifting the box a little to illustrate.

"Friday-night treat," she replied. Perhaps the initial shock of seeing each other was over, or the casual atmosphere of the pizza place helped, but he seemed slightly more approachable now than he had at his appointment. Which still didn't say very much.

"Ham and pineapple?"

"Still my favorite," she replied, feeling ridiculously flattered that he'd remembered that tidbit of information.

They stood there like statues, exchanging the most basic of pleasantries, an air of discomfort between them.

"Miss? Your order is ready."

She took the box, shifting her hands from the hot bottom to the sides. "Fresh from the oven."

And still they stood awkwardly, until Jonas chuckled.

She hadn't realized she'd been holding her breath until she let it out at the sound of his soft laughter.

"This is a hell of a thing, isn't it."

"It is." She started for the door and he followed her. It was easier for him to relax, she reasoned, her forehead wrinkling as she frowned. He wasn't the one carrying a secret around.

"There was a time when we weren't uncomfortable with each other at all. I don't know why we are now. That's all in the past. I didn't even know you'd still be here after all this time."

His words contradicted his cold manner of their first meeting and she wondered at it. "I stayed," she answered, hitting the door with her hip to push it open.

Jonas held the door and then followed her out, putting his white pizza box down on the hood of his truck. "I just go where they tell me."

Shannyn paused, the heat from the pizza warming her fingers. That had always been the problem. He was at the mercy of wherever his superiors sent him next. He'd done his training here, at Base Gagetown, finished when he was twenty-two. Still so young, full of energy and determination to be the best shot in the Army. Then he'd gone to Edmonton, and who knew where he'd been since then. Who knew how long he'd be stationed here? Despite his injury, it was obvious he was staying in the military, not looking to be discharged. That meant more moving around.

"And where would that be?"

He smiled but it seemed grim, a thin line. "Here and there. Doing what I do…what I did," he corrected himself. "I went where I was needed."

The very level of danger she'd worried so much about lent a sense of the mysterious to him, and Shannyn felt a glimmer of awe. He would have performed each task as it was assigned, no questions. For some strange reason, despite his aloofness, she knew what she'd always known. There was something heroic about Jonas Kirkpatrick. Something that made her feel safe. That was odd, because right now he was her biggest threat and he didn't even know it.

"What are you doing on base now? When you left you'd just finished sniper school." She looked up into his eyes. That had been a bone of contention in the end, too. An extra degree of danger that he'd relished and she'd feared. And it looked as though she'd had good reason to worry. He was only wounded. How many hadn't come back alive?

His jaw hardened, only slightly but enough that she saw it. Saw his eyes cool until they seemed to shut her out completely. In a matter of a few seconds, he had fully withdrawn into himself.

"I'm back at the school."

"More courses?" She couldn't imagine what else they would want him to do; he'd already accelerated through basic and had set his eyes on Special Forces. He'd obviously done his job and done it well.

"I'm instructing, sniping and small arms."

Her eyebrows lifted. Now he was in charge of training the next generation of sharpshooters? No more active duty? Had his injury caused that? How had it happened? She had so many questions and no right to ask. No right to pry. They were exes only, as far as he was concerned.

And truth be told, curious as she was, even though she still felt that *pull* to him, she knew it would be better for everyone if they kept things very impersonal. Getting involved in his life meant he'd get involved in hers, and she couldn't let that happen. For all she knew instructing was a temporary position until he could return to active duty. The last thing she needed was Jonas temporarily involved in anything and then leaving. She'd been through that enough in her lifetime.

"Do you like the new job?" She asked the question to fill up the awkward silence that had fallen.

His eyes didn't warm, just seemed to assess her distantly.

When they'd met six years ago, he'd been outgoing, fun, ebullient and full of life. It was hard to reconcile that energetic youth to the hardened man before her. The gulf between them now was wider than it had ever been.

"It has its good points."

Despite his earlier attempt at lightening the atmosphere, it was clear Jonas wasn't in a social chitchat sort of mood anymore, and it was just as well.

"Then I'm glad. I should get home."

"See you around."

She gripped the pizza box with one hand and looped her key ring around the index finger of her other. "Goodbye," she replied, surprised to feel her throat tighten.

It would have been easier if he'd just stayed away. She could have kept the memories of their idyllic months together untarnished. Now they were bookended with an image of a colder, harder man who seemed familiar yet a stranger.

She didn't need a man. She'd proven that. But if she were to choose one, it would be someone devoted, dedicated and, above all, present. Committed.

She couldn't imagine Jonas as any of those things.

\* \* \*

The leg press moved smoothly, up, down, up, down. Jonas grimaced at the weight on the bar. Ridiculous. It was half of what he'd been able to press only a year ago. He had enough reminders of what had happened to him without dealing with his body giving out.

He set his teeth and stubbornly added five more reps to his set, until the muscles quivered all the way up to his hip.

Tomorrow was his next physio appointment, and he was determined to have made progress. Everyone said his expertise and experience were beneficial to the training program here. But he knew the real reason he was back. He could no longer work out in the field. People called him a hero. He knew better.

He knew it was his fault.

Jonas slid off the black vinyl seat and sat on the mat, his legs spread out in a vee. Slowly he leaned forward, stretching out the muscles he'd just worked, gritting his teeth against the pain.

He hadn't expected to see Shannyn, that was for sure. Even so, he'd done nothing but think of her as the transport flight came in on final approach. He'd only been here in the Fredericton area for basic training, then sniper school. A small wedge of his life so far. But during that time…Shannyn had been a big part of that, and he wasn't immune to remembering happier days. She'd never been far from his mind.

But that was before. Before war, before deployment, before everything. Before the pervading taste of dust and blood. He could offer her nothing now, and he didn't want to. That part of his life was over, and he was moving on in the only direction he knew how. Within the Army. His home.

He lay down on his back, crossed one ankle over his knee, and drew the knee in, stretching out his hip. They'd run into each other twice already, and he'd been back less than two weeks.

Switching legs, he sighed. Tomorrow he'd go to his appointment, and then he'd see about switching therapists, go to another office. The less they saw of each other the better. For both of them.

# CHAPTER TWO

JONAS arrived for his appointment a few minutes early, providing the blond receptionist, who wasn't Shannyn, with a letter before seating himself in the waiting room.

"Shannyn?"

Shannyn, just entering reception, shook her head, diverting her gaze from the back of Jonas's head to the cheerful face of their receptionist, Melanie. "What is it?"

"It's Sgt. Kirkpatrick's letter. He wants his file sent to another clinic. He wants to switch therapists."

Shannyn took the file. "Thank you, Melanie. I'll take care of it."

Her even tone betrayed nothing of what she felt. Truthfully, she wasn't sure of it herself. Part of her was disappointed he wanted to go somewhere else, but mostly she felt relief that she wouldn't have to see him on a regular basis. The more she saw him, the more likely she was to be reminded of how she'd cared about him. Cutting down the risk of bumping into him could only be a good thing, right?

Then why did she suddenly feel so disappointed?

Shannyn unfolded the paper and stared at the writing. When she reached the end she looked over at him in the waiting area. He turned, meeting her eyes, his face unreadable. She wondered if they taught them how to perfect that look in the Army. In his letter, he hadn't offered any explanation for the switch. But then he didn't need to, did he. She got the message loud and clear. He didn't want to be anywhere near her.

The question she did have, however, was the one that she couldn't seem to get out of her mind. What had happened that made him only a whisper of the man he'd been six years ago? Where had that gung-ho, save-the-world optimist gone? Where had Jonas left him behind?

His file was already pulled for his appointment, and she went to retrieve it. It might be her only chance to discover what had really happened to him, and more than anything, before their brief contact was cut off, she wanted to know.

She opened the beige cover, staring at the documentation. So little information, just facts and figures and terminology that said very little about what had happened to the man.

He'd sustained his injury eleven months ago, but his file didn't say where or under what circumstances. The absence of data only made her more curious. He'd been stabilized, but the location had been blacked out. She'd had no idea there'd be such secrecy, and she looked up again at him sitting in the waiting room.

*Where have you been, and what have you been doing that's so dangerous it has to be classified?*

She continued reading. The file only stated that he'd been airlifted to Germany where he'd had surgery for a broken femur. Spent time there before being sent home to Canada for recuperation and rehab.

She read further, absorbing notations about the complicated operation to repair the bone and also about an infection that had delayed recovery.

He hadn't had an easy go of it.

It was probably enough to change a man. If combat hadn't

changed him first. She couldn't shake that nagging thought from her mind.

"Sgt. Kirkpatrick?" Even now the name seemed that of a stranger. She took a deep breath. "May I see you for a moment?"

His uneven gait carried him back to the counter. "Yes?"

Shannyn forced her voice to remain professional, even as she looked up into his face. He looked the same as he had last week. That inherent neatness and military bearing, despite his disability. She had the irrational longing to reach out and lay her hands on his lapels, straightening an imaginary crease. She shook off the silly urge. It would serve no purpose. If she were sure of one thing, it was that Jonas wouldn't stay around. She'd been burned by him before. There was no way she'd let him do it to her again.

She gripped the papers in her hand. "There are a few things I need you to authorize before I can sign off on your file and send it to the office you've specified."

She handed over the proper papers and a pen. "You should be fine there, although I think Ms. Malloy is the best physiotherapist in the city. Still, once this is taken care of, all you'll have to do is call and set up your first appointment at the new clinic."

Jonas's hand paused over the papers.

"Why you? I thought you were the receptionist."

She smiled thinly. When he'd been sent to Edmonton, she'd just enrolled in business school. "I started out that way. Now I'm the office manager. Any paperwork needs to be signed off by your therapist and by me."

"Sgt. Kirkpatrick? I'm ready for you now." Geneva Malloy called him in.

His eyes darted up to Shannyn's but she didn't let her gaze waver. She wanted him to sign the papers and be free to go on his way. On the other hand, they were running behind schedule and she didn't want to keep Geneva waiting. "I'll hold on to these," she said brusquely. "You can sign them after your session."

He handed her back the pen. She tapped the papers into an orderly stack and laid them on top of his file.

"Thank you," he replied politely. For a flash, his eyes betrayed him and she felt he wanted to say something more. Why, after all this time, did her heart still leap every time her gaze met his?

Then the look was gone and he limped his way to the facilities in the back.

She left his paperwork on the desk behind the counter and turned her attention back to her computer. This was her job, and had been for a long time. She'd done just fine, going to school, making a new life. She'd told him the truth—she'd started by answering phones and had gone on to manage the entire office. It was a good life. It was real and it was permanent and those were two things that Shannyn rated highly.

She turned her attention to her work while he was with Geneva. Checking her watch, she realized he'd been in there nearly an hour and her spreadsheet was complete. She sat back in her chair and sighed. Shortly he'd come back out, walk out the door and unless fate was unkind, she probably wouldn't meet him again. Being near him at all stirred up too many feelings she'd tried hard to bury.

Switching physiotherapists was a godsend. She could get on with her life, and he'd never know the difference. Even as she thought it, a slick line of guilt crawled through her. Most of the time she was successful in not thinking about what she'd done. But deep down she felt some remorse at keeping her secret.

The door to the back opened and she heard Jonas's voice talking to Geneva, thanking her politely. Shannyn turned her head toward the sound, only to snap it back abruptly as the front office door swung open carrying laughter with it.

"Mommy!"

A charged bundle in jeans and a red T-shirt barreled across the floor towards Shannyn's desk, bouncing to a halt and grinning up precociously. "Surprise! I came from kindergarten!"

Jonas released Geneva's hand as he turned, his heart stopping for a brief moment as the girl wrapped her chubby arms around Shannyn's neck.

*I have a daughter.* The thought struck him like the sure aim of a bullet.

As if she sensed something was off, the girl turned her head and their eyes met, green to green. Every muscle in his body tightened with the impact of the truth. *This is Shannyn's daughter. She's in school. I left six years ago. She has my eyes.*

Shannyn's cheeks colored; the blatant guilt on her face and the way she shifted in her chair seemed to confirm his suspicion. This was his daughter, one Shannyn had kept hidden from him all this time. A tiny poppet who looked eerily like the pictures of himself he remembered from his grandmother's photo album.

All of it left him gutted. How much more could he lose? He clenched his fingers. It wasn't enough to have the life he'd made for himself ripped away in the space of a moment. Now he had to find out he had another, separate life that he hadn't even known existed.

It took every ounce of his self-control to not go to the little girl, to kneel before her and demand to see her eyes again. Moss green eyes. His eyes in a miniature of Shannyn's delicate features. But what would that accomplish beyond frightening the child? She wouldn't understand. *He* didn't understand. No, it was Shannyn who owed him an explanation.

That overriding thought filled him with tense rage. And explain she would. She'd known. Known all this time and hadn't told him he had a daughter. For six years he'd been a father. She'd deliberately kept it a secret, and then when he did return to town, she'd said nothing, even though she'd had opportunity. This was the third time they'd met and still she hadn't breathed a single word of it to him.

Shannyn felt as if her head was moving in slow motion. Her daughter's happy, smiling face looked up at her. Then, turning her head a few degrees, she caught Jonas watching her with a startled expression blanking his face. Emma turned to see what she was looking at and lifted moss-green eyes to the man standing across the room.

Her heart raced even as the moment froze. He would know now for sure. There was no mistaking those eyes. Her own were aqua blue, and the only reason her lashes were dark was because she'd put on mascara that morning. Emma's eyes were his. Green with lovely thick dark lashes that curled naturally. Just like the brown curls that rested on the tips of her shoulders, the same sable color as his short spikes. She could almost see him mentally counting back six years.

Emma looked from Shannyn to Jonas and then to her baby-sitter, who stood in the doorway looking confused.

"Why's everyone standing so still?" Emma's voice piped up curiously in the silence that had fallen.

Shannyn shook herself out of her stupor. She forced a cheery smile to her face, the skin tightly stretched under the false expression. Right now she had to ignore Jonas and deal with Emma. Lord knew Jonas would have to be dealt with later.

"What brings you here in the middle of the day, pumpkin?"

"I told Melissa that I wanted to see you when she picked me up from school."

Shannyn reached down and lifted Emma up so that she was

on her knee, aware of Jonas's eyes on them unwaveringly. "And how *was* kindergarten today? Did you have fun? Learn the secret of moonbeams? Solve the mystery of the dinosaur?"

She made jokes, but her stomach churned with anxiety. He must have put two and two together by now. If not, he would have left the office. No, he knew exactly what the deal was. That they had a child and she hadn't told him.

He would hate her. This wasn't how things were supposed to happen at all. He was supposed to be switching therapists. Out of her sphere of existence. So she and Emma could live their lives as they always had.

"Mommy, that's silly."

She forced a smile as Emma's bright voice brought her back to the present. "And so are you, girly-girl."

"Can you come home?"

Melissa, Emma's sitter, stepped forward, holding out her hand for Emma to take. "I thought you were coming to run errands with me? We need to let your mom finish work." Melissa had sized up the situation, and had ascertained something was wrong. "We'll meet her at home later."

"Give me a hug, honey," Shannyn said, squeezing the tiny waist tightly against her. She blinked back the tears that threatened, already sorry for the changes she knew were coming to Emma's life. She'd hated the upheaval she'd experienced as a child; had tried to protect Emma from going through the same thing. Now, in the space of a few minutes, all her intentions were blown to smithereens. She gave Emma a little squeeze, wanting to hold on to her and keep the inevitable from happening. "Thanks for coming to see me. I'll be home soon, okay?"

The response was a smacking kiss on the cheek. "See you later, alligator."

It was Emma's latest funny and she never seemed to grow

tired of it. "In a while, crocodile," Shannyn called back, her throat tight.

When the whirlwind had departed again, Shannyn braved a look up at Jonas.

"We need to talk." She heard his voice and the tight quiver of anger it carried. Trembling, she made her gaze remain on his, no matter how his tone intimidated her. He ignored the other faces in the waiting room, his eyes piercing hers, accusing. She'd lied to him, and right now she knew that was all he could see.

"We need to talk, Shannyn, *right now*."

Shannyn's heart quaked. It would have been too much to ask that he not see the resemblance. She'd spent so much time telling herself that he'd never find out that she wasn't prepared for this conversation.

"I'm working. We can talk later, Jonas."

His voice was nail hard as it bit back. "We can do this here, with all these people around, or we can go somewhere more private, but Shannyn—we're talking *now*."

Carrie stood behind her, and Melanie picked up the phone that jangled in the stillness, shattering Shannyn's nerves. There was no way on earth she and Jonas could talk here. And by the way his lips were thinned, she knew prevaricating further would be a mistake. Plain, unvarnished truth would be the only way to explain. They had to get out of here, somewhere neutral. She looked into his face, all hard angles and unrelenting anger. He was furious, and she knew she didn't want to be completely alone for this conversation. She needed the protection of somewhere public if she were going to make him listen to her.

"I'm taking the rest of the afternoon off," she said to Carrie in an undertone. "If you need anything over the weekend, e-mail me."

"You go," Carrie murmured back. "And call if *you* need

anything. I mean it, Shan. Anything." She looked over her glasses meaningfully at Shannyn.

Shannyn grabbed her purse and nodded at Jonas. "I'm taking the rest of the afternoon off."

He followed her out the door.

They stepped out into the June sun, and Shannyn squinted against the glare. She'd left her sunglasses on her desk, and she could really use them now, both to cover her eyes and to put some distance between her and Jonas. Hostility was fairly emanating from him, and she had no idea how to defuse the situation so they could actually have a conversation. One where he might understand why she'd done what she had.

When they reached the sidewalk, he grabbed her arm none too gently and guided her across the street, past the old barracks and down to the Green.

Shannyn shook his hand off when they reached the grassy expanse, taking a few steps away from him. He hadn't hurt her. But her hopes at an amicable conversation had evaporated when the firm grip of his fingers dug into her skin. Even though he wasn't holding her arm anymore, she felt his animosity. His jaw was clenched tightly and he walked—no, marched—across the grass, assuming she'd keep up with him.

He was angry, and had every right to be. Right now she had to pick her battles. How she dealt with him now would affect everything that happened from this moment on.

He stopped beneath an elm, shoved his hands into his pockets and stared out over the glittering water of the river. Shannyn held her breath, waiting for the explosion, not knowing what to say, wondering what his first words would be. She was grateful that they were in a public place. It would preclude a shouting match, and perhaps the presence of others would make him more willing to listen. If she were lucky.

But the words wouldn't come. When she remained silent, he spoke. Not with anger, not with a shout. With a quiet certainty.

"She's mine."

Shannyn nodded, surprised at the sting of tears that filled her eyes at the simple statement, the moment of truth. This was the father of her baby. A man she'd once loved. A man who was all but a stranger now. She tried to focus on the sailboat gliding down the river, but the image blurred.

"What's her name?"

"Emma."

She made herself turn and look at him, face this conversation head-on. The time of evading was done. His Adam's apple bobbed as he swallowed. But he wouldn't look at her. His face remained stoic, expressionless.

"Emma is my grandmother's name."

"I know."

"Why did you do that?"

Finally he turned his head from the river. His eyes glowed like polished jade in the shade of the elm.

How could she explain without it seeming more than it was? The truth was she knew how much the Army meant to him. His grandfather had fought in World War II and died. If Emma had been a boy, Shannyn had been going to name him after Jonas's grandfather Charles. Paying tribute to the wife Charles left behind seemed the next best thing. At the time, it had been the one and only way she planned on connecting her child to her father. Making sure a little bit of Jonas lived on in his daughter. Perhaps she had also done it to assuage what guilt she had at her silence.

"I know how much you love your gram." She went with the simple explanation.

"Loved. She died two years ago."

The lump in Shannyn's throat grew, making it difficult to

swallow. So many changes, for everyone. Time didn't stand still. "I'm sorry."

Jonas walked away, finding a nearby bench under the elm and bracing his elbows on his knees.

She gave him a few minutes, taking the time to calm herself so she could control the conversation. If that were possible.

She'd done what she thought was best. She also knew Jonas wouldn't see it that way. She'd wanted to protect Emma. Emma deserved more than a part-time father. More than a dad who would only be around when it worked out with his schedule. She didn't need a dad out of obligation. They'd been dating when Emma was conceived. She'd known the moment he'd said he was shipping out that he wasn't interested in a lasting relationship. If he had been, he would have asked her to wait, or asked her to come with him. When she'd discovered she was pregnant, two weeks after he was gone, she knew she couldn't tell him. He'd already qualified as a sniper. He'd be in danger every day.

Jonas hadn't wanted more with her, and she hadn't wanted a man who stayed only because he'd been trapped into a role he hadn't expected. She'd been a product of that sort of relationship and had seen the devastating consequences of pretending. She'd known from experience that eventually it would have crumbled, and Emma would pay the biggest price. Shannyn had vowed then and there to never put her daughter through that sort of pain.

# CHAPTER THREE

JONAS looked over at Shannyn, watching her bite her lip, worrying it. She'd changed. He hadn't realized how much when they first re-met. But she was a mother now. A mother to a child. A child he'd never known existed. His child. It was hard to reconcile the fun-loving girl he remembered with this woman who seemed so remote and unfeeling. Because her not having told him was cold, and she would never convince him otherwise.

How could she have done that to him? He wanted to reach out and shake her, demand to know what she'd been thinking. Hear her paltry justifications.

Instead he rubbed a hand over his face, struck once more by the image of a curly haired poppet with his eyes, vibrant and excited. A huge argument wouldn't accomplish anything, and he knew it. But keeping his cool outwardly didn't stop the shock or the anger pulsing through him.

He'd never wanted to be a father. But finding out he was one, knowing she'd kept it a secret, made his blood boil. What had he ever done that was so bad she thought to punish him in this way? The fact that she wouldn't have said anything if she hadn't been caught only fueled his anger.

"You shouldn't have done it," he finally ground out through his teeth. He kept his voice as level as he could; too many people were around and he didn't want to make a huge spectacle. "You had no right to deny me my own child."

Shannyn moved a step or two closer. "I can explain."

Jonas stared out over the river. How much time had he spent in this very water during his training? How many times had they gone boating or swimming, feeling the cold slickness of the water on each other's skin? How had things gotten to this point? How could it be that they were in this place again, strangers dealing with something as intimate as a shared child?

His heart pounded as memories flooded back, unfaded by time. When had Emma been conceived? On a day like today? Years ago, on an afternoon like this, he would have found a secluded spot downriver. He would have made love to her there in the heat of the afternoon. Things had burned hot between them from the very beginning. And fires that burned hot usually were extinguished just as quickly.

Only it hadn't. It had smoldered all this time in his memories of her.

He had good memories. Memories of the two of them together during a summer that had been more than a fling. Memories he'd kept tucked away, bringing them out only when the pressure got to be too much. Memories that were now suddenly tarnished by a gigantic lie.

"Nothing you can say will justify keeping this from me."

"Please Jonas, just hear me out."

"Hear you out? What can you possibly say that will make this right? I left for Edmonton six years ago. And you knew you were carrying my child and let me go anyway, none the wiser."

His hand automatically found his thigh, rubbing it absently as he'd had a way of doing since his injury.

"I didn't know I was pregnant when you left."

The defense rang false. "Don't give me that. You would have

found out within a few weeks. You knew where I was stationed, knew my battalion. You could have gotten in touch if you'd wanted."

She came closer and sat on the opposite end of the bench. "You're right. It was my choice not to tell you."

"Why?" He thought briefly of how his grandmother would have loved seeing her great-granddaughter, her namesake, and the single word came out thick with emotion as anger and loss poured through him in waves. It was a struggle to keep his voice steady and low. He was glad she was sitting closer, so not every person wandering the walking path could hear the sordid details.

"There were lots of reasons. For one, you left me. You never once said you wanted me with you. I knew if I told you and you came back, it would be out of obligation and not a...deeper emotion."

"I had my reasons," he bit out. He knew she was referring to love. He hadn't said it back then, hadn't wanted to.

"I'm not saying you were wrong. I'm saying what I based my decision on. Let's face it. If you'd wanted more from me, you could have called. Or sent a letter. You left and I never heard from you again."

"You're blaming me?" He couldn't keep the incredulity out of his voice. Somehow she was making this his fault? Just because he hadn't said *I love you*? He'd lost his daughter for five years because she felt *spurned*?

"No, Jonas, of course not." Her words came faster, and he sensed her desperation. "But what I am saying is that our situation, our personal status, wasn't one that supported the idea of us and a baby. I knew you didn't want marriage and a family. And I wasn't about to put Emma through what I went through as a kid. Divorce sucks."

She sighed and softened her tone. "But that wasn't the only factor."

"Go on."

He met her eyes as she folded her hands in her lap. Good Lord, she was beautiful. Maybe even more so now than she'd been then. Her blond, streaked hair was gathered up in a clip, the ends falling in artful disarray. Her eyes were blue and clear as a morning sky over the Arabian Sea. Her skin was sun kissed and dotted with light freckles.

He'd been enchanted back then, not knowing she'd have the ability to do something like this to him. It irked him to find that he still responded to her girl-next-door sort of beauty, even when he was as angry as he'd ever been in his life.

"Oh, Jonas, look at you," she lamented, her lips downturned as she struggled to explain. "You were young, we both were. You were in the military, on the fast track to Special Forces. I knew it. You would be moving around all the time or deployed. And what would we do when you were gone for months at a time? Wait for you to come back, perhaps more of a stranger each time? A part-time father for a daughter who didn't understand why Daddy wasn't around? Or worse—what if you didn't come back at all? I didn't want to give my daughter a father only to have him ripped away from her in some foreign country."

"So you took her away from me. Denied me the chance to know my own flesh and blood."

"I protected her!"

"From me! From her father!"

"Not from *who* you were. From *what* you were."

Heads turned in their direction as their voices rose. She took a deep breath, spoke more calmly and tried a different tack. "Did you want to be a father then? Be honest."

He paused, clamping his lips together. Of course he hadn't. He'd been twenty-two, at a brand-new posting with a new stripe on his sleeve. He'd been well on his way to becoming the best shot in the regiment. He'd had his eye set on deployment and making his mark. And as much as he'd cared for Shannyn, the last thing he'd wanted was to be tied to a wife. A family. He'd had things to accomplish first. A wife and children had no place in that world.

"That doesn't mean I didn't have a right to know."

She turned away so she was staring at the lighthouse in the distance. "I did what I thought was best for my daughter."

"Our daughter."

Even saying it felt foreign on his tongue.

How had his life come to this? Back where he started? He stretched out his leg, trying to relieve the ache that settled in his quadricep. Why couldn't things have just stayed the same? Being with the battalion. Doing what he did best. Being the best.

He stared ahead. He could see Chris's face before him still, wide and smiling after cracking some joke. The two of them running laps around the compound before the desert got too hot to breathe. The quiet, reassuring sound of his voice while Jonas stared through the scope.

Their last mission:

*The taste of dust was everywhere.*

*Parker's voice was low beside him telling him to hold his shot. The midday sun beat down harshly, and Jonas wondered if it was possible to bake in one's own skin. He held his position; sweat trickled down his neck, sticking to his skin, but he didn't move a single muscle. Hadn't moved for the past three hours, twenty-seven minutes and fifteen seconds. "We've got someone at the door, Park."*

*"It's not him. Not yet."*

Godforsaken desert, *Jonas thought, biding his time. He'd been in the desert long enough that he was sick and tired of it. There were nights when he lay awake for hours, thinking of home. Of cold beer in a sports bar and a bacon cheeseburger, instead of army chow and warm water from his canteen. Instead of dusty roads and the same unending landscape as he traveled from assignment to assignment. At least he had Chris Parker to keep him from going crazy.*

"Jonas? Jonas, are you okay?"

Shannyn's voice broke through, and he turned his head slowly, surprised to see her sitting there beside him. She reached out to touch his arm, and he flinched. She drew her hand back automatically, her blue eyes suddenly troubled.

"I'm fine," he answered roughly. The flashes of memory were happening more and more frequently, and always at the strangest times. He couldn't seem to control them. They were always, always of that one day. Bits and pieces here and there that hit without warning, leaving him feeling raw and exposed. It always took him some time to reestablish himself with his surroundings.

"You don't look fine." Her voice was low with concern. He hated that tone. Hated it every time someone looked at him the way Shannyn was looking at him now. As if he didn't quite make sense.

"I said I'm fine," he snapped, rising to his feet and taking a half-dozen steps to get away from her. Faces turned again in his direction, and he took deep breaths to try to get his heart rate to return to normal. He wished the memories would all go away so he could get on with what was left of his life. Only, now that too was thrown into chaos by learning he was somebody's father.

Shannyn stared after him, warning bells pealing madly in her head. What was going on?

They'd been talking and then suddenly he'd gone. His eyes had blanked and every muscle in his body had stilled. It had been eerie, watching him disassociate, until she realized his breathing was accelerating.

She'd tried to call him back, and the empty stare she'd seen before he came to frightened her more than anything else.

What in the world had happened to him?

She was getting in far deeper than she cared to. Now that he knew Emma was his, naturally he'd assert his rights and demand to see her. She couldn't deny him that. And seeing him this way, knowing something was horribly wrong, she could already feel herself being drawn in. Wanting to help him almost as much as she wanted him gone.

What if he shouted this way at Emma?

When he turned back, she fortified herself with all the courage she could muster. "This is a perfect example of why I didn't tell you. Emma is five years old, Jonas. She's not going to understand if you blank out and then shout at her. She's not equipped for that."

She wanted to say that, even as an adult, she didn't understand him either, but right now the focus had to be off her own feelings and on keeping Emma safe and happy.

"I have a right to see her. She has a right to know me."

"Why is this so important to you? Why can't you just let it go?"

"Because she's my daughter. My responsibility." His former control reasserted itself. "I'm not the kind of man who shirks responsibility. I thought you understood that much about me."

"That's what I'm saying." Shannyn implored him with her hands. She did understand. As much as she was hurt that he'd left her, she'd admired him for his dedication to what he considered his duty. And he would have been dutiful to Emma too and it would have broken her heart little by little to know that he was staying for that reason and not of his own free will. Would have destroyed her to come home one day to a man who wanted out. Who wanted a life away from her and Emma. She never wanted Emma to feel abandoned and unloved the way she had felt growing up.

"You would have stayed involved out of responsibility, not out of any lasting affection."

Jonas looked around them. Now that the shouting was over, no one seemed particularly interested in their exchange, no one noticed anything out of the ordinary. People simply walked along the path, enjoying the early-summer day, the mellow heat, the fresh green of the grass and leaves. Everything seemed to spin in a slow circle. The desert, Germany, the base, all spiraling outside of *here*. A perfect world around him while he felt trapped in chaos. His whole world was changing. It didn't seem real.

He clung to the one thing he hoped she might understand, searching for common ground that would anchor him to this unreal situation. "Shannyn, you've brought her up alone. I could have helped."

"With child support." Her lips thinned to a straight line.

"Well, yes."

Her short laugh surprised him. "And your money would have made it all right."

"It might have lessened your financial strain. It couldn't have been easy."

"We've done just fine, thank you."

Jonas stared hard at her—dismissive. Her tone, her body language…it was all dismissive. He wasn't wanted or required here. God, he wasn't really wanted or required anywhere anymore. In a world of doers, he was now redundant. What had once been his purpose was gone. And he'd never thought about what he'd do when it was over. He'd always thought he'd keep doing what he was doing until he died on some battlefield. He certainly hadn't expected to come home with a gimp leg, leaving him good for next to nothing.

He saw the talent in the next wave of elite soldiers and hated that he wasn't one of them anymore. Put out to pasture at the ripe old age of twenty-eight. It didn't seem fair. He'd lost his career, and now he discovered he'd lost a family he hadn't even known he had.

"I want to see her."

"I'm not sure that's a good idea."

His eyes blazed. "Shannyn, you can't keep me from my own daughter."

"I'll do what I have to, to keep her safe and happy."

"And you think I'd threaten that?"

"She doesn't need a temporary dad who'll leave once he satisfies his curiosity."

That was what she thought of him, then. It showed how little she knew. How far apart they were.

"Look at me," he whispered stridently. "Does it look like I'm going anywhere? You've seen my file, right? Active duty is a long shot at best, out of my realm of possibility, more likely, according to the doctors."

He stepped closer, close enough that she had to tilt her neck sharply to look into his eyes. Her chest rose and fell rapidly, so close he could almost feel it against his. His gaze fell to her lips, and they opened slightly. How he could despise her so much right now and still want to kiss her was beyond him.

"I'm obviously not in danger anymore. So tell me, Shannyn. What is it you're really afraid of?"

# CHAPTER FOUR

SHANNYN took a step back. "You're invading my personal space."

Jonas laughed, a brittle sound as he stared at her with accusation in his eyes. "I beg your pardon." He affected a small bow, mocking her, and put more distance between them.

"You can't keep me from my daughter anymore," he argued firmly. "And you know it."

Shannyn's heart sank. He was right. Now that he knew about Emma, she had no right to keep him from her. Legally she had no reason to deny him visitation. All she had were her own reservations, which would matter very little in the overall scheme of things if he pressed his case. She decided to appeal to whatever sense of fatherly concern he might possess.

"I don't want her upset."

He put his hand into his trousers pocket and tilted his head, watching her closely. "Neither do I. I'm willing to let you name the terms of how we do this. Within reason."

"You are?" It was the last thing she'd expected from him and she couldn't keep the surprise from her voice.

"You can tell her about me by yourself, if you wish. And we'll meet wherever you think she'll be most comfortable." He balanced his weight on one leg and smiled thinly, a smile that seemed forced and manufactured for the moment.

"Thank you," Shannyn breathed with relief.

"I don't have any desire to traumatize her, Shannyn." His jaw softened slightly. "I'm not in the habit of terrorizing children."

"Of course not." She dropped her eyes. After the initial blowout, he was suddenly being remarkably reasonable. Appealing to him from Emma's point of view had been the right course. He was exerting his rights, but at least he wasn't blind to how this would affect Emma.

"You have the weekend." He straightened, putting his weight equally on his feet once more. "I'll be in touch Monday, and we'll talk then about how to move forward."

She met his gaze again and clenched her fingers. He was making it sound like a business transaction, or an assignment.

"For someone who says I can handle this how I want, you're being awfully dictatorial. It's not some battle plan you've concocted."

"I just want to make sure you don't drag this out. It's been six years. I think I have a right to have doubts about your...*expediency.*"

Shannyn felt as if they were right back to the beginning of the argument again, and she didn't want to rehash everything that had been said—and unsaid.

"Fine. But just so you know," she lifted her chin, "bossing me around really isn't going to help your case any."

Jonas stared down into her eyes, and she struggled not to feel intimidated. In front of her now was a man accustomed to getting what he wanted. One who gave orders and had them followed. One way or another. But she *was* going to do this on her terms. It didn't matter what it took, she'd go toe-to-toe with him, for Emma's sake. Protecting herself right now came second to making sure Emma remained unhurt through everything.

She got the feeling the battle was going to be draining. In more ways than one.

"The weekend, Shannyn." The words were softly spoken, but she was left in no doubt of the ultimatum they contained. "I'll be in touch on Monday."

He spun on his heel and walked away, his gait lopsided from his injury.

Shannyn went back to the bench and sat down heavily. How on earth was she going to find the words to tell her baby that she had a daddy after all?

She chose the backyard because that was the place Emma was most comfortable and happy. They didn't have a huge yard, but what they did have was lush with green grass and a perfect place to play. A white fence separated them from the neighbours, and in one corner Shannyn had put a small flower bed and herb garden, as well as Emma's outdoor toys.

Today Shannyn felt the need to be outside in the fresh air, not cooped up in a room where she found it hard to breathe. Every time she thought of what she'd say to Emma, her heart faltered. In her mind she'd gone over and over the questions Emma might have, and how she'd answer them so a five-year-old would understand. She'd thought about it so much that here it was Sunday afternoon and still she hadn't done it.

But Jonas would call tomorrow. She was sure of it. And if she hadn't told Emma by the time he did, she knew Jonas would make things very difficult.

"Honey, you want a Popsicle?" Shannyn called out to Emma who was pumping her legs and swinging on the secondhand swing set Shannyn had bought at a yard sale last spring.

"Okay." The legs stopped pumping, and the swing slowed until Emma popped off and landed on the grass.

It felt more like August than June today. Mellow warmth soaked through Shannyn's T-shirt and heated her legs. It was the kind of day that made her wish she were out boating on the river, or lying on the beach at the lake. For a minute she got caught in memories of Jonas, a Jonas who was less jaded and more carefree, squidging his toes in the sand at the beach as she lay in his arms.

But reality was that she was supposed to be having a life-altering discussion with her baby, who wasn't so much of a baby anymore.

She handed over the Popsicle and patted the seat of the picnic table.

Emma hopped up and Shannyn smiled down on her dark head as she licked the Popsicle. Everything she'd done in these past years had been for Emma. To give her the kind of life every child deserved. One filled with love and fun and, most of all, stability. Different from the one she'd had. Her number-one priority had been to protect Emma. To do what she thought was best. Now she had to undo everything with a simple conversation. Turn her little girl's life upside down.

How did she even begin?

She hadn't said anything at all until Emma started preschool and began noticing her friends had mommies and daddies. Or that they lived with their mommy and saw their daddies on weekends. When the question arose, she had given Emma the short version. That her daddy didn't know that she was born and that Shannyn didn't know where he was right now. And then she'd reinforced how happy and good their life was. It had never been her intention that Emma would find her life lacking in any way. And Emma had accepted her answers like any young child would. With trust.

How could she now explain that her father was here and wanted to see her? In her heart, Shannyn knew he would leave again. Maybe not next week or next month, but eventually he would leave and Emma would be fatherless again. How was that fair? She put her hand on Emma's curls, feeling the warmth radiating from her scalp. Every single decision she had made had been to protect Emma from upheaval.

"Mama? Can I play on the slide now?"

Shannyn looked into her daughter's eyes. They were so like Jonas's and since she'd seen him again they seemed even more so. Being with him, even through their arguments, only served to remind her how much she'd invested in him so long ago. And how much she'd invested in their daughter in the years since.

In the end she couldn't give the words voice. "Yes, you go play, honey." She took the empty Popsicle stick from Emma's sticky hands and kissed her cheek. Emma went back to playing, and Shannyn watched from the table. And for the first time since she'd found out she was pregnant, she really had no idea what she was going to do.

"What time's your lunch?"

Shannyn knew the voice even though the words were clipped and economical. He didn't waste any time. Nine-fifteen and he was calling already.

"I get a break from twelve until one."

"Meet me at the lighthouse at noon."

"But, Jonas, I…"

She heard loud noises slamming in the background as he cut her off. "I've got to go now, but twelve o'clock at the lighthouse." Shannyn heard a voice shout in the background before the line went dead.

Her hands trembled, not with fear but with anger. He said he was going to let her handle this, but all he did was make demands left and right. When to tell Emma. When to meet. She should ignore his latest order and stay right where she was. But that meant he might come to the office and confront her there, and a public scene was unacceptable for their clients. Damn him for putting her in such a position.

He was expecting her to tell him that Emma knew about him and plan the next step. It would have been easier to tell him over the phone rather than face-to-face. There was no way she could explain it so that he would understand, but she was going to have to try.

She was waiting outside the white-and-red structure, looking over the water when he stepped up behind her.

"We're in for some showers."

She turned and caught her breath.

He was wearing his trousers but his shirt was missing and he stood before her in an Army-issue T-shirt. And, oh, he filled out every cotton inch. Flat where everything should be flat, a wide chest and broad shoulders that led to arms with muscles that dipped and curved. His boots gave his six-foot-plus frame even more height. His size made him more attractive to her, not less. She wished she didn't find him attractive at all. All that lean fitness, paired with his handsome, if uncompromising, face, was a tempting combination. Not tempting enough to make her forget how he'd hurt her, though. Thankfully his interest at the moment was focused on Emma and not her. One complication was enough.

She swallowed, chilled by the sudden puff of cool air preceding the dark cloud coming down the river. Goose bumps shivered up her arms and she folded them around herself as thunder rumbled low, still miles away. Even though the sky directly above was blue, the water seemed discolored and white caps dotted the surface.

"Yes, it looks that way," she managed to reply.

He held out a brown paper bag. "I know I hijacked your lunch break, so I grabbed something on the way."

Shannyn stared at the bag, recognizing the familiar logo. "You didn't."

A smile crept up his face and she realized it was the first time he'd really smiled at her, a smile that connected. It moved from his lips and thawed the ice in his eyes as he admitted, "Of course I did. You can't get a hamburger like this overseas, heck, not even in Edmonton. And I brought lots of napkins." He held out his other hand, revealing the white stack.

He led her up the steps to one of the benches that lined the perimeter of the lighthouse, then reached into the bag and handed her the foil-wrapped sandwich. "I got extra cheese on yours."

Shannyn smiled back, secretly pleased that he remembered another one of her favorites. She hadn't had one in ages. Sliding the foil pocket back slightly, she took her first bite and sighed in appreciation at the juicy beef and tang of the condiments.

"Mmm." She let the sound vibrate through her lips as she swallowed and put the sandwich down on her lap. "I haven't had one of these in a long time."

"We used to eat a lot of them, way back when."

She used her napkin to dab at her lips; it was a tasty but messy business. She wrinkled her eyebrows. She was surprised he'd made such a casual reference to their past after the resentful tone of their last meeting. For a brief moment as their eyes caught and held, she got that tumbling in her stomach, a lifting and turning that she'd almost forgotten. Perhaps it was brought on by nostalgia of what had been, but not completely. Part of it was a pull to the man beside her now. Tall and strong and more than a little enigmatic. A man who made her wonder what was simmering underneath.

"Yes, we did," she responded, the words coming out slightly breathy.

"It was a good summer."

That summer had changed her life. And not just because she'd gotten pregnant. But because it was the first—and only—time she'd been in love.

They'd met through mutual friends at an outdoor concert in Officers' Square. Right away she'd been attracted to the lean, dark-haired boy who seemed to have so much energy.

They'd started dating, and things had progressed rapidly. It had been a whirlwind, magical.

But the young man who had captivated her heart and enjoyed life to the full and made her laugh, was gone. She supposed they'd both grown up. But his smile and the brief memory took her back. Made her wonder what it would take to bring that smile back again.

She watched him as they ate for a few minutes in silence. He was more relaxed right now. Perhaps it would be a good time to get some answers to her questions. And not just for Emma. For herself. She wanted to know what had happened in the years since that summer. What made him tick. When her curiosity got the better of her, she asked the question that had been plaguing her.

"What have you been doing the past six years?"

His chewing slowed. He looked away as he admitted, "I made Special Forces. I was there until nearly a year ago."

"Where were you stationed?"

"I moved around a lot. Wherever I was needed."

"You won't tell me."

He looked back at her then, and she realized the soldier was once again in control. "I can't tell you. Sometimes I was sent with a regular Recce platoon."

He saw her confusion and elaborated. "Reconnaissance. We'd offer support to operations, that sort of thing. Other times…" He paused, his gaze slipping from hers again. "It doesn't matter now, anyway. Those days are gone."

Shannyn folded her hands and watched his head turn away from her. She got the feeling it mattered a great deal. "It changed you, Jonas."

"Being in combat changes everyone." He still refused to look at her, instead appeared to be people watching.

She didn't know why he felt the need to generalize everything so much. "I'm sure it does. But I'm interested in how it changed *you*."

"Why?"

Ah, a question with several answers, some she'd acknowledge, some she wouldn't. She picked the only one that was relevant. "Because you are Emma's father."

Whatever was left of his lunch he wrapped up and put back in the bag.

"Whatever it was I thought I knew that summer, I was wrong."

"Wrong how?"

He balled up the bag and got up, taking a small hop on his good leg to right himself before depositing everything in the trash can. "I was full of myself and what I was going to do. I was indestructible. I thought I knew everything." He sighed heavily. "And I really had no idea."

"You hardened." Shannyn held her breath waiting for his response. She could sense his stubborn withdrawal and couldn't help but see the resemblance between him and Emma, especially now when he seemed so unhappy. His lips seemed fuller; the bow shape of his mouth so much like her daughter when she'd had a rough day at school or got overtired. He'd passed on his fair share of traits whether he knew it or not, and it drew her to him. How could she hate the man who had given her such a precious gift?

When his answer came it was not what she expected.

"I know I've probably seemed hard and demanding. I'm sorry. I've lived in a world where you give and receive orders."

The small confession touched her. "You don't smile anymore. Or at least not like you used to."

His eyes pierced her and she wondered if he was trying to see her thoughts.

"You've changed, too. You're cautious. Reserved. And for what it's worth, you don't smile much, either."

"Maybe we just don't smile at each other." It was out before she could think about what she was saying, and she bit her lip.

"Perhaps we should try." He sat down again at the table. "I'm trying to look past my resentment of you for lying to me. For Emma's sake. What did she say when you told her?"

Another gust of cold air hit them, and Shannyn brushed a piece of her hair away from her face, lowering her eyes. The thunder that had been creeping up the river rumbled closer, and the first lightning pierced the gray sky.

"I didn't tell her."

"You what?"

His earlier geniality evaporated. The hard edge of his voice was matched only by the thunder that boomed. The first cold droplets hit her skin, and Shannyn looked at the path of the storm. She could only see perhaps half a kilometer away; farther than that was a gray curtain of rain.

"We've got to get inside," she exclaimed, thankful for the temporary diversion.

"Are you kidding?" Everyone who'd been outdoors was suddenly scrambling for shelter. The lighthouse, really a museum, was already filling up with tourists. "My truck's parked on the street. We can make it if we run."

Heavy drops of rain marked the path as they jogged toward his pickup. Jonas reached the vehicle first and unlocked her door before running around the hood to the driver's side and clambering in just as the skies opened up.

For a few seconds the only sound was the drumming of rain on the roof of the truck and their heavy breathing.

Jonas rested his hands on the wheel, picking up the conversation where it had left off, much to her dismay.

"You didn't tell her. We agreed."

"No, you demanded. You said I could do this my way and then you ordered me about like one of your privates. Which I am not."

His only response was the use of a very indelicate word.

Shannyn straightened her back and half turned on the seat. "I'm the mother of your child and perhaps you should remember that."

"You're right. How could I possibly forget something that has happened so *recently*."

Embarrassment bloomed in her cheeks at the acid in his tone. He was never going to forgive her. "Look. I tried, I really did. But I just didn't know how to tell her. How to answer the questions she's sure to have. Can't you understand that?"

"You had no trouble with the decision not to tell me. What have you told her about her father, anyway?"

Shannyn looked at the windshield, but saw nothing but water streaming down the glass. "I told her you didn't know that she was born and that I didn't know where you were."

She felt his eyes on her, condemning.

"Now that was a bit of a lie, wasn't it. Because you could have found me quite easily if you'd tried."

"Does it really matter now?" She sighed. "There is no point belaboring what has or hasn't been done."

"Convenient for you."

Shannyn snapped her head around at the contempt in his tone. "I beg your pardon, for trying to find the best way to tell our daughter that you are here now. For trying to find the way to explain things that will cause the least hurt and confusion. She's five, Jonas. Five. If I need an extra day or two to do that, then you're going to have to deal with it. What if she asks why you left me in the first place? Why you didn't care enough to stay?

What am I supposed to tell her then? That your precious Army was more important than we were."

Her lower lip trembled slightly as emotion overwhelmed her. Her cheeks flamed hotly at what she'd revealed in her outburst. It didn't take great powers of deduction to realize that a good part of her decision had been based on her own feelings of abandonment.

"I don't know what you tell her," he answered. "But you know as well as I do that your last statement isn't quite accurate."

She didn't know what he meant. Whether it was the part about the Army being more important or the fact that he couldn't have chosen the army over them because he didn't know there was a "them." The straightness of his body, the way his eyes blazed at her, kept any thought of clarifying it at bay.

"But I know two things," he continued after a moment. "I know you want to be the one to tell her, and I know that you're the one who got us into this whole situation and you are going to have to work it out."

"Why do you even want to be involved in her life?"

Jonas gripped the steering wheel. Why indeed? He wasn't happy; he knew that. He had a permanent limp, and he was a single man in the military.

But none of that mattered because he was now also a father. And surprisingly, that seemed to carry more weight than anything else. He stared at the rain streaming down the window as he answered.

"Because I am her father. Because I missed out on her first five years. I didn't get to see her as a baby, or watch her first steps, or hear her first words. I didn't get to help her on the school bus on her first day of school or put a Band-Aid on her bumps and bruises."

He stopped, turned his head and met her eyes. The aqua-blue eyes of the woman he'd once loved, who now didn't understand anything about him at all. "I missed all of that, Shannyn, and I missed it because you thought it was 'best' not to tell me. And I'm sure about one thing. I am not going to miss out on any more of her life. She is my daughter. I am her father. She is a part of me whether you like it or not. And I agreed to let you tell her in your own way. I *trusted* you to do that. It appears I misplaced my trust."

Shannyn lifted her chin. "You haven't inspired a whole lot of trust yourself, Jonas."

He took his hands off the wheel, turning his body so he was angled on the seat. He winced against the sudden spurt of pain in his thigh. She thought he'd betrayed her in some way when he'd left her. Maybe that was just as well. They were certainly miles apart now.

"I will see Emma. You will tell her about me and we will, together, come up with a time and place for me to meet her. Because if that doesn't happen, Shannyn, you'll force me to take legal action."

All the color dropped from her face, and he regretted that he'd had to resort to such tactics. He wasn't sure if he could even go through with such a thing. He knew it made him sound cold and unfeeling. And he wasn't. The problem was he felt too much these days. Felt so much that at times it overwhelmed him. He pushed away the emotion. She was the one forcing his hand, not the other way around.

"You wouldn't," she breathed.

"I would," he returned. "Don't test me on this, Shannyn. I want to do this amicably. I really do. But that's up to you now."

The windows had steamed up, and he started the engine, cranking up the defrost button. Within seconds a circle of clear glass expanded until he could see outside. The rain was moving downriver and he turned on the wipers, clearing off the windshield.

"Buckle your seat belt. I'll drop you off at the office."

When he pulled in front of her building, he put the truck into Park but left the engine running.

"I'll expect your call very soon, Shannyn. If I don't hear from you by the end of the week, you'll be hearing from my lawyer."

She got out and slammed the door without saying anything.

He pulled away from the curb, heading back to base. He was determined to get to know his daughter, and he was willing to threaten her with lawyers and judges to do it.

But he hadn't counted on how much it would hurt—not just to fight with Shannyn but to spend time in her company.

# CHAPTER FIVE

"HONEY, remember the man at my office the other day?"

Shannyn closed the book she'd been reading to Emma and snuggled the pajama-clad body close. She couldn't put this off anymore. She had no doubt that Jonas would find a way to see Emma, and it was her job to make sure Emma was okay with it. More than okay.

"The tall one that looked at me funny, right?"

"Yes, pumpkin, that man." Shannyn wasn't surprised Emma remembered; she had a sharp memory. "I have something to tell you."

Emma turned her face up at Shannyn expectantly. Shannyn didn't know whether to smile or cry. How could she make Emma understand something that she herself did not? This perfect little face, the creamy skin of youth, devoid of the lines of worry that came with age and a loss of innocence. Lines like the ones she'd seen around the corners of her own eyes lately.

Shannyn had done everything she could to protect Emma, and yet here they were.

"Emma, that man…" She paused, tucking Emma close. Her voice caught on the rest of the sentence. "That man is your daddy."

Emma pulled away slightly and her mouth opened. "My daddy?"

*Oh, honey.* Shannyn took a deep breath, willing the right words to come.

"Yes, pumpkin. He didn't know that you were born, so seeing you…well it was a surprise to him."

"He didn't know I was a baby?"

"No, sugar. His job took him away before you were born. But—" and this was the hard part "—he wants to know you now."

"Mama," Emma whispered, a smile broadening her face at the brilliant news. "I thought he forgot."

Shannyn wrinkled her brows. "Who forgot what, honey?"

"Santa. Last year I asked him for a daddy but I didn't get one and so I thought he forgot."

If ever there were a moment that Shannyn truly regretted what she'd done, this was it. She'd thought she'd done such a good job as a single mother, but knowing that her precious baby had asked Santa Claus for a daddy broke her heart. She only hoped that somehow Jonas could live up to Emma's expectations.

"He wants to meet you, Emma. But I don't want you to get your hopes up too high. Jonas doesn't know what it's like to be a dad, and I don't think he's been around kids much." Shannyn paused, wondering what sorts of people Jonas *had* been around over the years. "I don't want you to think this is going to be perfect, okay? We need to take it one day at a time."

But Emma's joy was undiminished. Her eyes shone as she rose up on her knees to give Shannyn a kiss. "I can't wait!" she said before falling back on the couch and hugging her arms around herself. "A mama *and* a daddy," she murmured, fully pleased.

The tears and questions Shannyn had anticipated never came, but Emma's blatant, unvarnished enthusiasm worried her even more. What if it all went wrong? Where would Emma be then?

Shannyn rotated her neck, trying to work out the nervous kinks that had settled there. All her careful planning and her years of justifying her decision to herself were about to become reconciled in the next half hour.

She fussed with a tray on the breakfast nook table. Thankfully the showers of the week before had moved on and the skies were clear and pure. Today had been the last day of school for Emma; she'd been done at noon, and Shannyn had taken the afternoon off. She was so nervous enough about tonight that she wouldn't have been able to focus at the office anyway. Jonas was due any moment. And she was going to introduce him to his daughter.

She looked through the patio doors at their picnic table, the red vinyl tablecloth flapping gently in the light breeze. Metal clips anchored at the corners kept the cloth from blowing away. An end-of-school barbecue had seemed the best idea.

"Mama?"

Shannyn looked away from the window and down at Emma. Her little girl was dressed cutely in a denim skort and red T-shirt, her curls pulled up in a bouncy ponytail.

"Yes, pumpkin?"

"Does my daddy like hamburgers?"

Shannyn's heart caught. Emma's wide eyes looked genuinely concerned that perhaps her new father wouldn't like what was for dinner, and Shannyn's returning smile was slightly wobbly as she knelt down before her.

"Don't you worry. Jonas—" she still couldn't seem to bring herself to say "your daddy" "—loves burgers." She tipped Emma's nose with her finger. "I think he even likes pickles almost as much as you do."

Emma's smile was bright as she skipped away outside to play on her slide. Shannyn, however, couldn't help but frown. As rational as Shannyn had tried to be with her, she hadn't been able to contain Emma's innocent enthusiasm. There was so much potential for Emma to be hurt when she had such expectations.

"Shan?"

She started at the sound of her name. When she spun in response, they both froze. The absurd impulse to rush forward to his arms sluiced through her. Years past they would have done just that. He would have pulled her close and kissed her, let his hands…

But not now. It was only the surprise of his sudden appearance that made her fancy such things. Now he kept his distance, his very presence larger than life as he stood in her kitchen.

"I knocked but no one answered. I let myself in."

She took a fortifying breath. She'd been so lost in her worry she hadn't even heard him drive up. "Sorry…"

Whatever she was going to say evaporated from her mind. Gone was the military-issue clothing. In its place he'd worn jeans and a T-shirt in a gray-blue color. Out of politeness he'd removed his shoes at the front door and was in stockingfeet. His hair was always the same, but the relaxed dress brought him down to a level of greater familiarity, and Shannyn remembered all too vividly the times they'd spent together when he'd been out of uniform. Walking the beach, he'd dressed in board shorts and T-shirts, or going to clubs he'd worn jeans that hugged him and made every woman in the room thank the good Lord for the rear view.

"Are you okay?"

She tried a light laugh that came out as a nervous twitter. "I'm fine."

He looked down at himself and back up at her. He had yet to smile, and she hoped he could muster one up for Emma's sake.

"I thought this would be better than the uniform. More approachable."

He'd been right on that score. Shannyn wondered what kind of shape he'd been in *before* his injury, if he still remained this lean and fit now, a year later. His casual clothes emphasized his slim hips and muscled upper body.

"Just be careful with her," Shannyn warned. She had to put some distance between them because seeing him in civvies was affecting her more than she liked. It was bad enough that Emma had her heart set on a new, perfect daddy. Shannyn had to be the voice of reason in all of this and couldn't afford to forget that, just because simply seeing him cranked up her pulse a notch or two. In the end it changed nothing.

"Of course I will. I would never hurt her, Shannyn. You must know that."

*Maybe not intentionally,* Shannyn thought, but pursed her lips together.

Jonas was nervous, Shannyn realized, seeing how stiffly he held his body. It would probably be better for everyone if they got the introductions over with and dealt with whatever came next.

"Why don't you get your shoes? Emma's in the backyard, and we've planned a barbecue." When he'd departed for the front door again, Shannyn pressed a hand to her belly.

Jonas had no idea what it meant to be a father. He certainly wasn't prepared for what Emma would throw at him. Despite Shannyn's best efforts, Emma was expecting a ready-made, perfect dad. One that perhaps smiled once in a while. And what did Shannyn expect out of this? If it didn't work out, she'd have to deal with Emma's disappointment. And if it did, she'd have to deal with Jonas on a permanent basis. Neither option held a lot of appeal. Seeing him was a constant reminder of how much he'd hurt her.

When Jonas came back grim-faced, shoes in hand, Shannyn let out a huff.

"For God's sake, Jonas, could you muster up a smile? You don't need to frighten her half to death."

He stilled, sucking in his lips and letting them roll out again to their natural shape. She couldn't help but watch the movement, struck by a memory of how soft yet firm they had been years ago when he'd kissed her. When she let her gaze roam upward, his eyes had darkened from their usual green to a deeper hazel color.

They only did that when he was upset, she remembered.

"I'm sorry," he replied gruffly. "I'm…I'm just nervous."

"You're scared of a little girl." Shannyn couldn't help the smile that curved her lips. "You, the big bad soldier."

But her teasing didn't help banish the anxiety from his face. "This is different," he said simply.

It made her feel a bit better. At least he wasn't treating this cavalierly. "I'm just saying—" She tempered her sarcasm, keeping her tone even and gentle."—Emma is a very open, loving child. She's not going to understand if you're cold and distant."

Jonas stared down at Shannyn. Sometimes she seemed almost the same as she'd been…like the other day when they'd eaten lunch together. Approachable, warm. At those times he remembered all too well what it had been like with her before. When her smile had been just for him, making him feel ten feet tall and bulletproof.

At other times, like right now, he felt he didn't know her at all. And while he wanted to meet Emma, he felt totally unequipped to handle the challenge being thrown his way—to be a happy, loving father. How was he supposed to do that when he'd all but forgotten what love felt like?

"I don't know what to do," he admitted.

Her face softened, and the gentle way she laid her hand on his arm felt foreign. But good. Suddenly they were connected again, and as his eyes met hers he was shocked to realize that he wasn't imagining the link between them. The one that would

have been there, Emma or no Emma. It almost felt uncompli-
cated. But that was crazy. There were scads of complications
between them. Those she knew about and those she didn't.
Hopefully never would.

"Just say hello. Smile. Tell her you're pleased to meet her.
She'll help you with the rest."

Jonas figured Shannyn knew Emma better than anyone, and
he pulled away, already missing the feel of her hand on his skin.
"Let's go." He slid his shoes onto his feet while Shannyn opened
the patio doors.

The heat hit him first, the steamy humidity of a June afternoon. Inside the cool house, he'd momentarily forgotten how hot
it was outside until the wall of it hit him. He thought for a
moment how it was a very different kind of heat from that in the
Middle East.

It was a lifetime ago; it was yesterday.

He shook himself from his thoughts to hear her calling Emma
from the swing set.

The bundle that came running was the liveliest picture he'd
seen in years. A flawless vision of life and innocence, and the
purity of it struck him square in the chest. She ran across the
grass, a bouncing tail of curls and arms and legs that had not quite
lost all their baby chubbiness, still perfect in their youth.

His heart stopped when she smiled and called out, "Daddy!"
as she ran directly for him.

He wasn't prepared, and she hit him full force in his bad leg.

Her tiny arms were wrapped around his hips as the muscle
quivered and buckled completely, taking him to his knees on the
grass. Tears stung the backs of his eyes as Emma let go and
stepped backward, shocked—the big, strong man brought to
utter humiliation by a tiny squirt of a thing. The pain was nothing,
nothing compared to the shame he felt.

"Oh my God, Jonas, are you all right?"

Shannyn's worried voice reached his ears and he inhaled deeply, nodding. Emma was staring at him with something like fear and guilt paling her tiny face. When he looked up at her, she choked a little and started to run to the other side of the yard, to the pint-size playhouse by the far fence.

"Emma." Shannyn started toward her but Jonas stopped her. "No. Let me."

He got to his feet, hopping a bit on his good leg so he could get steadied. *Introduce himself and pleased to meet you, indeed.* All the good intentions for a smooth transition were annihilated. He ignored the pain radiating from his thigh up through his groin and even to the pit of his stomach. Taking a deep breath, he took the first painful steps toward making things right with his daughter.

When he got to the playhouse, he looked inside and saw her sitting on a small bench, her knees pulled up to her chest and her delicate lips turned down in a perfectly inverted *u*. Tears glimmered like emerald drops in her eyes.

"Emma?"

She looked up. The playhouse was too small for him to go inside. He tried squatting by the door and the pain took his breath away. He finally rested his weight on his knees, bracing his hands on the miniature wood door frame.

"Emma, I'm so sorry for what just happened. It's not your fault."

"I hurt you," the words came, tiny and contrite.

The knowledge that she blamed herself touched him. He knew how that felt, only in his case, the self-blame was deserved. But Emma hadn't known of his wound, he was sure of it.

"No, honey, you didn't. I was hurt a long time ago, and you didn't know. It was bad luck that you grabbed the wrong spot."

"How did you get hurt?"

Jonas swallowed against all the pain that came with that

question. Being here now was heart wrenching enough. How did he explain it all to an innocent girl? One who deserved a more perfect world than the one she was inheriting?

"I was in an accident about a year ago. It was a long way away from here and I was in the hospital for a few months. And it is getting better. Now I just have to exercise and keep seeing the therapist. That's why you saw me at your mommy's office."

"Oh."

"I'm the one who's sorry, Emma. I think you feel bad and that makes me sad. I wanted us to meet and be happy."

Emma's eyes cleared and her knees came down from her chest. "Me, too."

He held out his right hand as if introducing himself. "Let's start over. Hi, Emma. My name's Jonas and I'm your daddy."

He hadn't known how those words would actually make him feel until he said them. They cracked the shell he'd constructed around his heart, letting in little beams of love. He was someone's father. She was a part of him. And she was beautiful.

She rose from the bench and took his large, callused hand in her smaller soft one. "I'm Emma. I'm pleased to meet you, Daddy."

When she smiled she looked like Shannyn. So much of him was in her looks, but the smile and the freckles were all Shannyn. He shook her hand gently.

"I think if you were to try hugging me again, you wouldn't hurt me."

When her arms went around his neck he put his around her and squeezed.

So much over the past few years had convinced him that life was devoid of hope. Of beauty. Of tenderness. Somehow, by some miracle, one hug from his unknown daughter changed all that. Because in her embrace he knew beauty and tenderness and most of all, the elusive glimmer of hope.

When they released each other his smile was genuine. "That was a first-class hug," he praised. "Now, I think your mom is probably worried about us. Let's go back and get this barbecue underway. I think I saw hamburgers."

He pushed himself to his feet, took her hand in his, marveling at the innocent trust in the simple clasp, especially after he'd frightened her so. Together they walked back across the lawn toward Shannyn.

Shannyn had waited for them to return from the playhouse. She must have decided not to come after them, because as they turned the corner of the playhouse she took only a few steps forward and halted. Emma held his hand, walking slower than usual in deference to his contracted gait.

Shannyn's fingers lifted to her lips. He could see the tremble there, could see the soft shine of tears on her lashes, and for a moment he forgot about his injury and all the reasons why it was wrong. For a few blissful seconds he was the man he'd wanted to be for her, all those years ago.

For a brief flash, the bitterness of the past disintegrated and he felt larger than life. Like a man coming home to his family. A child's pure handclasp and a waiting woman.

It wasn't just Emma who was bringing back to life the feelings he'd locked away. It was Shannyn. He understood her wariness and fear. He'd experienced his share of it. Right or wrong, she'd made her choices and now she was having to deal with the consequences, and the strain showed on her. But in those moments when she forgot, she was the Shan he remembered. There'd been times when their eyes met that he felt sure their connection was still strong.

He had no clue how he was going to maintain a relationship with his daughter while keeping Shannyn at arm's length. He wasn't the man for her. Not anymore. He'd made his choice and to change his mind would only be unfair to her. He wouldn't make promises he couldn't keep.

What woman would want half a man? He couldn't help the limp that took him closer to her with every step. What woman would choose such a man? Even one who had never forgotten what it was like to love her?

As they reached the patio, he wished for the first time that they could go back. But there would be no going back. She'd broken faith with him with her lies.

He looked down at Emma, holding his hand with the simple trust of innocence. Somehow he and Shannyn would have to find a way to work through this. He was here now.

Shannyn blinked back the tears that had gathered as they approached. She'd been wrong, she realized. Jonas had said it but somehow she hadn't believed him. She'd thought her reasons had been justified. But seeing them together now, their hands joined, the beam of pure bliss on Emma's face, only slightly brighter than the one on Jonas's... She shouldn't have kept Emma from him all these years. She should have told him and dealt with the consequences, then and there, instead of putting it off, pretending it would never happen.

"Mama, this is my daddy," Emma announced as they met Shannyn in front of the patio blocks.

"We've met." Shannyn tried a smile, but it quivered.

"He was hurt and I didn't know, so that's why I hurt his leg."

Shannyn got the meaning behind the strange five-year-old logic and nodded. "I know, sweetie. I should have told you; warned you to be careful."

Emma held his hand firmly in his. "That's okay, Mama," she responded. "Daddy 'n' me? We're good."

Shannyn couldn't help but laugh, even through the emotion

thickening her throat. At times Emma sounded so much like the toddler she'd left behind, and at other times the adult tone told Shannyn she was growing up fast.

"I'm glad. I think we can start cooking the burgers now. Do you want to set the table, Emma?"

"If Daddy helps me."

It was going to take a very long time for Shannyn to get used to the word *Daddy* coming out of Emma's mouth. "Maybe Jonas can pour the drinks while you put out the plates."

For several minutes dinner preparations were ongoing, and Shannyn was thankful for Emma's happy chatter, telling Jonas about school and her friends and what her favorite toys were. It filled up the awkward silences that would have happened. When they finally sat down to eat, Emma passed Jonas the plate of sliced pickles first thing.

"Mama said that you like pickles almost as much as me."

Jonas took the plate and raised an eyebrow at Shannyn. A slow smile flirted with the edges of his mouth. "I do. I'm surprised she remembers."

Emma brushed it off. "Oh, Mama, she remembers *everything.*"

Shannyn felt Jonas's eyes on her, and heat infused her cheeks.

"Does she now," his soft, knowing voice answered.

Oh, she did. She remembered things she knew would be far best forgotten, no matter how his smile or the sultry sound of his voice played havoc with her good intentions. Just because Jonas was back and involved with Emma, didn't mean there was room in her personal life for him.

Perhaps she'd been wrong in deciding not to tell him he had a child, but the reasons she'd done it were still there. He hadn't loved her then. He hadn't once contacted her after he'd transferred. Nothing between them had changed since then. She hadn't been enough, and they were even farther apart now. Nothing he'd said or done since coming back gave her the impression that anything would be different a second time around.

And she knew she wouldn't survive a second time.

But it didn't stop the remembering. She remembered how it felt to lie in his arms and look up at the stars. The touch of his lips on hers, the feel of his hard muscles beneath her fingertips.

When she shook herself from her reverie, Jonas was looking at her strangely.

It would be best if he didn't know the direction of her thoughts. Because somehow she had to keep him at a safe distance.

# CHAPTER SIX

WHEN dinner was over, Shannyn sent Emma inside to change into her pajamas while she cleared the table. To her surprise, Jonas wordlessly gathered plates and took them into the kitchen.

Shannyn came back through the patio doors, folding the red-and-white tablecloth as she went. Everything had its place here. But then, she'd always felt the need for order. Perhaps it was the lack of structure she'd had growing up, once her mother left and her father had raised her alone. She'd had to take it upon herself to provide some sort of home life, but she'd only been a child. Her father hadn't put in much effort, either.

By the time adulthood came around, Shannyn had known what she'd always sensed during those difficult years. She wanted a home. A stable, secure, consistent environment. She'd been ready to settle down as Jonas had been getting ready to explore what he'd thought were bigger, brighter horizons.

She watched Jonas open the dishwasher, loading it with the dirty dishes from the counter. Quietly she passed by him and tucked the tablecloth into a drawer. Jonas might look the picture of domesticity right now, but she knew he'd been carted from pillar to post as a child as the son of an army major. It had never seemed to bother him, moving around from one place to another.

Shannyn had made a home for herself and Emma, something permanent, and it was yet another thing that kept them apart.

He put the last plate in the rack, added detergent from the cupboard beneath the kitchen sink and started the cycle. Shannyn wondered how he felt about it now, knowing he probably wouldn't face deployment again. Was he looking forward to less travel, or would he miss it terribly? Did he dread being sent from base to base for the remainder of his career and missing out on the action?

When he finished and turned back around, she avoided his eyes, keeping her hands busy by fussing with a dish towel. Jonas wouldn't stay; she knew that. But for Emma's sake she was glad he didn't face the same level of danger he always had. At least she should be able to avoid *that* conversation with her daughter.

In the quiet of early evening, with the mess tidied up, Jonas's next words were a surprise.

"She's a wonder, Shannyn. You've been a great mom. I can see that."

All her senses seemed to tingle as she tried to exit the intimate working area of the kitchen. "Thank you."

His hand caught hers as she passed by.

Shannyn looked up, her blue eyes pleading with him not to make this more than it was. "Don't. Don't do that."

She tugged her hand free, but he didn't let the matter drop. "Do what?"

"Pretend this is something it's not."

"I only spoke the truth."

He dismissed her concern, and Shannyn tried to tell herself it had been a compliment and a casual touch. But her cheeks flamed as his eyes remained steadily on her face. She hadn't been mistaken about the connection she'd felt earlier. A part of her wanted to explore it, to see if it was still as strong as she remembered.

A bigger part, the broken part of her, told her to leave it alone.

That they were all better off if he went his own way. Or at least kept his contact with her in reference to their daughter only. She wasn't prepared for more from Jonas. She couldn't harden her heart and enter into something she knew ahead of time was temporary. It would be a huge mistake, and she needed to keep both eyes open. Even she understood that much.

"I'm just being honest. She is a bright, happy little girl and I have you to thank for it."

"Even though I kept her from you."

"Yes, even though." He shoved his hands into his pockets.

"You're not angry anymore that I lied to you."

"I didn't say that."

Shannyn sighed, going to the table and resting her hands on the back of a chair. She couldn't expect him to forgive her just like that. The fact that they could even discuss it now without argument was progress. Progress she didn't want to sabotage by throwing blame back and forth. It would accomplish nothing, and Emma would be in the crossfire. After listening to her parents argue for years, she refused to repeat that pattern with her own child.

"You…you were great with her. Thank you."

He took a few steps closer, so that his voice rumbled, the seductive sound raising the fine hairs along her arms. "She made it easy. I'm sorry about how things started out." His apology was genuine. "If I had have anticipated…"

His words trailed off but she picked up where he'd finished. "I didn't see it coming, either. I knew she was excited. I should have been more prepared."

"I don't know how we could have been prepared for this."

His words hung in the air between them. "This" meant more than coparenting. She'd be a fool to think that it didn't also mean the growing attraction between them. If she was feeling it, it was possible he was, too. Despite all the reasons they were angry and resentful toward each other.

"Me, neither. I should have thought of it. I'm awfully sorry, Jonas."

Shannyn kept the topic on track but couldn't help but think how odd it was that they were discussing their child's welfare while she was upstairs changing into her nightgown. To do so after six years of no contact whatsoever. To see him, hear his voice, feel the brief touch of his fingers after thinking he was gone forever.

"She's not going to understand when you have to leave again." Shannyn grabbed the stack of paper napkins from the holder and started folding them into triangles. Anything to keep her hands busy. "She doesn't understand how the military works like I do."

"What do you expect from me? I can't help that assignments change. I go where I'm needed. And in my current condition, that's here." He pointed to his leg. "I have a constant reminder of where my life has led. It doesn't stop me from being her father. It's not my fault we're in this mess."

She heard the bitter tone in his voice and wished he didn't feel so angry all the time. It was becoming clearer that he wasn't just mad at her. She was sure there was something deeper, something to do with what had happened to him. Perhaps it was how he'd received his wound. She didn't know and refused to ask. She only knew she couldn't shoulder all the blame.

"It's not exactly mine, either," she snapped.

"If you'd told me from the beginning…"

"Are you saying you'd have left the Special Forces? Stopped being a sniper? You'd have come home to change diapers?"

"I was deployed. The decision of where I'm stationed isn't usually up to me, Shannyn. Whether I like it or not."

Jonas clamped his jaw shut and stared past her shoulder. It had never bothered him before, going where he was told. Yet in the past few months he'd started to resent the choice being taken away from him. "Let's just say I don't know what the future holds for me and I'll deal with it when it happens," he finally ground out.

"That really doesn't help me prepare Emma, now, does it." She stopped her folding and finally faced him dead-on.

"It's the best I can do." He pursed his lips, resenting the fact that somehow they'd ended up arguing anyway, even though he had only wanted to pay her a compliment.

"And it's why I didn't tell you about her in the first place." Her eyes narrowed with accusation. "Did you know she asked for a daddy for Christmas?"

Of course he hadn't, but he couldn't help but warm at the thought. It fit with the impression he'd gathered of her today. He made another attempt at defusing the situation.

"Shannyn, we're all feeling our way around here. I've only just met her today. I don't have a fatherhood instruction book telling me what step to take next. And believe me…I have enough to deal with already."

But Shannyn was undeterred. It was as if she was pushing him to admit something. "Like what? You're working as an instructor now. That seems a pretty choice assignment for someone your age."

The simple mention of having to deal with things made his heart pound harder, faster. It wasn't a choice assignment. It was all he was able to do after having his leg mangled on a nameless battlefield no one was supposed to know about. He wasn't fit to do anything else.

"That doesn't mean I necessarily earned that spot. What do you want me to say, Shannyn? That I miss active duty? I'll admit it, freely. I was damned good at what I did and at least there I didn't feel…redundant."

"Passing your expertise on to others makes you redundant?"

"It's what they do when you can't do your job anymore." He spread his arm wide. "They find a place for you somewhere else. Reassign you to something in an office. Because you're not fit to serve your purpose."

It was out before he had a chance to think, and he realized how angry he sounded.

"You do that a lot. Say things but leave it so ambiguous it seems like a riddle. Why don't you explain what you mean."

That was the one thing he couldn't do. She looked at him differently now, and it would be even worse if she knew the truth. A sheen of cold sweat popped out on his forehead. He'd let his unit down. He'd let Parker down. And they'd given him a medal and called him a hero for it. But no one understood what he'd been through.

"Jonas?"

Shannyn put her hand on his arm. He'd gone again, just the way he had that other time on the Green. One second engaged in conversation, the next completely disassociated and so very, very still. Except for the nearly imperceptible trembling beneath her hand.

She didn't know what she'd said to prompt his withdrawal, but it was becoming clearer to her that there was something else going on with Jonas. Watching him disappear from the present was frightening enough. She didn't know if he blanked out or if he actually went somewhere else. To a memory maybe, one so potent it couldn't exist in the same space as the present. Despite her warnings to herself to stay uninvolved, it wasn't in her not to care.

Besides, it was in Emma's best interest. If there were something more going on with him, she had to know. If it frightened her, she couldn't expect a five-year-old to understand.

"Jonas. Are you all right?"

Slowly his eyes focused on her again. "What?"

"Where did you go just now?"

He slid his gaze away and she knew he was evading.

"Nowhere."

"Jonas." She refused to let him turn away when he would have, and she reached up to cup his chin. "Jonas, please let me help you."

Green eyes settled on hers as he pulled his head away from her touch. There was something different about him just at this moment, she realized. He seemed almost vulnerable, so different from the aloof hostility he normally used to armor himself. Perhaps now she'd be able to take advantage of a window of opportunity. Gain some understanding of what was really going on with him.

"You don't want to help me, Shan. Trust me."

But he used the shortened version of her name for the first time since returning, and it tethered them together. They both knew it. It didn't matter how many years were between them. Once his gaze connected with hers, it held. Clung. Like a lifeline between them.

"You should talk about it," she persisted. "You're so angry. I know there's more going on than just discovering Emma is yours. More than you being angry with me for keeping her from you. Not talking about it isn't going to make it go away."

"I wouldn't know where to begin."

Shannyn sighed and leaned against the front side of the counter, forgetting all about napkins and tablecloths and focusing solely on him. Jonas was weary, she realized. And not just from his injury. It wasn't physical. But inside, where it really mattered. And he was holding it all inside where it festered like an infection. He would only balk at tenderness. But a more logical approach…

"You need to talk about it, because right now I get the feeling you're having a hard enough time by yourself, let alone parenting a five-year-old girl." She folded her arms. "Now that you've met,

I know you're going to ask for time with her. What happens, Jonas, if you have her and you lose time the way you did just now?"

"I don't lose time."

"I just watched you. For nearly five minutes."

His jaw hardened, a muscle twitching beneath his ear. "You're using her to deny me access now."

Shannyn shook her head. "No, I would never do that. You know that. The last thing I want is to put her in the middle of some ridiculous struggle between you and me. For her sake, I want to help you."

She pushed away from the counter and went to him, laying a hand on his arm. His lack of response didn't faze her. "I'm her mother. Before you decide you're going to be a father, you need to act like one. And that means getting help for yourself when you need it, whether you want to or not."

Jonas heaved an exasperated sigh, and his chin jutted out stubbornly. It was a look Shannyn recognized in Emma and if she weren't so worried, the resemblance would have made her smile.

"What's it going to take to make you happy with this?"

The answers that raced through Shannyn's mind were varied and surprising in their complexity. She'd thought she was happy before he came back, but sometimes now it seemed as though he'd never gone, as silly as that sounded. She wanted Emma to be happy. She wanted Jonas to be a part of Emma's life, now that the truth was out. And she realized she might even want him to be a part of *her* life, even though she didn't see how that could ever happen.

He would always be the kind of man to run off chasing a new assignment, a new adventure. And she'd be the one left behind again. Wanting to be a part of his life and allowing it were two very different things. Knowing what she knew about him, and what would inevitably happen, made being attracted to him utter nonsense.

But they had to build some sort of bridge.

"A good start would be telling me how you were injured."

He shook his head, his chin jutting out farther. "No, I can't."

She raised her eyebrows, pulling her hand off his arm. "Can't or won't?"

"Right now it's the same thing."

"You're going to tell me it's classified, right?" She blew out a puff of air, lifting her hair from her forehead. "Convenient."

"The location is classified. The…incident…is a matter of record."

She watched him swallow, look at his shoes and then look up again. "I just can't, okay?"

She accepted it because it was obvious that pressing him would get her nowhere. Perhaps it would be better to work their way there gradually. "Okay, then, how about telling me about what happened when you left me and went to Edmonton?"

She instantly regretted her choice of words. His face closed off completely, all vulnerability wiped away until he had all the openness of a classified document.

"You make it sound like I chose the Army over you."

"Didn't you?" She asked the question without hostility. She already knew the answer. She turned to get the kettle, feeling the sudden need for the soothing effects of tea.

At that moment Emma reappeared, dressed in a soft pink nightie, her face scrubbed.

"You ready for bed, pumpkin?" Shannyn put the kettle aside and forced a smile.

Emma nodded. "My story first, please."

Shannyn took her by the hand and led her to the stairs, taking the first steps.

"Aren't you coming, Daddy?" Emma paused and asked the question over her shoulder.

The plea was heartfelt, and Shannyn let her gaze fall on Jonas, still standing by the kitchen counter. He looked so lost, a great giant without a country. But that was ridiculous. Jonas had always been the strongest man she'd known. She wondered what his answer would have been—about choosing the Army over her. The way he sometimes looked at her made her believe that he'd cared after all. That maybe he still cared a little. Just not enough.

The bigger question was, did she want him to care at all? Even if she had loved him then, his answer to her earlier question was of the greatest importance. If he hadn't cared enough to choose her then, what made her think he'd be any different this time? And could she take that risk with her heart after letting him break it once already?

He smiled but kept his gaze on Shannyn. Before her eyes he went from looking lost to having a purpose, and she knew it was Emma that made the difference. Her body warmed beneath his appraisal.

"I'd be honored, Emma. If your mama doesn't mind."

"It's all right."

His steps sounded behind hers as they climbed the stairs. It was an intimate sound. How many nights had she climbed these stairs alone, wishing for another's to echo behind her?

She tucked Emma in, all the while aware of his body filling the doorway, blocking the light from the bathroom. Standing guard as she read Emma's favourite book, *Love You Forever.* Waiting quietly as she tucked Emma in snugly and kissed her good-night.

She'd nearly made it to the door when Emma's voice stopped her.

"Aren't you going to tuck me in, Daddy?"

Shannyn made the mistake of looking up at him. His eyes widened with the wonder of being asked such a thing, as if he'd been given the moon.

"Okay." Hesitantly he stepped forward, smoothed the blankets about her, and leaned down to place a kiss on her forehead. "Good night, Emma."

"Good night," she whispered back.

Shannyn watched, swallowing against tears gathering in her throat. She'd missed him so when he went away, and had often wondered what it would have been like for him to know Emma, even while doing her best to protect her daughter. She still wasn't sure Jonas wouldn't hurt them in the end, but the tender way he was with Emma touched her deeply. It was like he put everything aside and focused on her alone.

He was here now. The more she saw of Jonas, the more convinced she was that he was dealing with something bigger than she realized. Perhaps Emma with her guileless ways could help with some of that healing. Perhaps in a way Shannyn couldn't seem to.

He turned from the bedside and Shannyn saw the glimmer of tears on his cheeks before he cleared his throat. When he passed by her, his hand squeezed hers.

She turned and followed him downstairs, expecting to talk. But when they got there, he merely mumbled a thank you and left before she could say anything.

Leaving her with more questions than she'd had when he'd arrived.

On Sunday, Jonas called on the fly, saying he was heading across the river on an errand and would Emma like to go for lunch.

Shannyn paused. On his first visit they hadn't even broached the topic of visitation—when and where he could expect to visit. Yet after his episodes, she wasn't comfortable in letting Emma go with him alone. He'd only met her once, after all. The alternative was that in order to say yes, she'd have to go, too.

She held the receiver close to her ear, knowing he was waiting for her answer. And wasn't this a slippery slope? If she wanted to keep her perspective, seeing Jonas should be the last thing she wanted. Instead, her heart leaped at the sound of his voice.

"I'm not sure that's a good idea," she explained. "Emma has only seen you once. I think it might be too soon."

"Then you come, too. I have to drop something off on Main Street, and I was going to grab some fast food. I thought I could use some company."

She didn't know what to say.

"Shannyn, you told me that you wanted me to be present in Emma's life, not in and out. That's all I'm trying to do."

Now he was using her own words against her. Keeping him at arm's length was proving more difficult than she'd imagined. "I don't know, Jonas, it's awfully sudden."

"Come on, Shan. It's only lunch. What else have you got going on today? It's Sunday. It's raining."

"I'm cleaning the house." She looked around at the living room, dusted and polished. A tiny white lie wasn't going to kill her.

"It's an hour out of the afternoon. I'd really like to see her."

Shannyn couldn't come up with a more-logical argument. "Oh, all right. Lunch, but that's it."

"I'll pick you up in half an hour."

Shannyn hung up the phone and frowned. The sudden urge to change into neater clothes came over her and she resisted. There was nothing wrong with her jeans or the cotton pullover she'd put on this morning. Her hair was up in a ponytail and she left it that way as a point of defiance. She was not going to make an effort to be *pretty* for Jonas Kirkpatrick!

Emma, on the other hand, decided primping was necessary, and the minutes leading to his arrival were spent picking out "the" right shirt and brushing Emma's hair until it shone. Shannyn tucked it back with a headband and couldn't help but smile at the pixie face grinning up at her.

"Where're we going to eat?" Emma asked.

"I don't know. You'll have to ask Jonas."

Emma held on to the stair railing as she bounced down the stairs. "I hope it's Wendy's. I'm going to have chicken nuggets and fries and root beer."

Shannyn only shook her head. Some days she wished she had a fraction of Emma's energy and enthusiasm.

"Put your coat on, Emma. It's raining."

She was helping with the zipper when she heard the slam of the truck door. "He's here. Best manners, now."

"Oh, Mama," Emma lamented at the reminder, making Shannyn laugh.

That was how Jonas saw them when she opened the door. Giggling like two girls sharing a secret. Shannyn's hair was pulled straight back into a ponytail and the remembrance of wrapping that tail around his hand and pulling her close slammed into him, making him catch his breath. Emma looked up at him expectantly as she stepped outside and on impulse he reached down and scooped her up.

He held her on one arm as he smiled at Shannyn. "Let's go. First one to the truck gets extra large fries." He shamelessly used the old taunt from their dating days.

Shannyn shut the door and took off at a run. He couldn't follow, and they both knew it. He was handicapped twice over, once with his leg and the other with the extra weight of Emma on his arm. She reached the vehicle and placed one pointed finger on the hood before snapping open the door and hopping in out of the rain.

Jonas leaned his head close to Emma's and whispered, "Your mama was always a pig about French fries."

Emma giggled and Jonas bounced her on his arm. It was probably wrong to tease Shannyn so, but he couldn't resist. Not when she opened the door looking exactly like the girl he'd fallen for long ago.

His heart told him that a date with his daughter and her mother was the perfect way to spend a lonely Sunday.

His head was another matter. Because it came through his consciousness loud and clear that spending time with Shannyn was a big mistake for both of them.

# CHAPTER SEVEN

THE buzzer sounded for the second time. Jonas lowered the towel from his head and anchored it around his waist with a hand. Whoever it was wasn't going away. He might as well answer it.

"Yeah," he barked into the intercom.

"It's Shannyn."

He paused, sighed. He'd thought the voice mail he left was clear enough. There was an air show this weekend and he wanted to take Emma. Shannyn too for that matter, if she still wasn't comfortable with him taking Emma on his own.

Their lunch had been fun, devoid of all the loaded atmosphere of his first meeting with Emma. Perhaps it was getting away from home, being in a neutral location. Or the fact that it was a brief outing with no purpose beyond lunch. Whatever it was, he'd enjoyed it. Enough that the air show seemed like a great opportunity. He could show them some of the birds he'd flown in.

Apparently his message hadn't been clear enough, because she was here now.

Shannyn would press him about things he didn't want to talk about. She wouldn't have forgotten his last episode. But it wasn't something he cared to discuss—ever.

He had to expect to talk to Shannyn now and again if he planned on being a part of Emma's life. He had to keep his thoughts away from what had been between them, because letting their past spill over into the present would only cause complications. If he could keep the topic of conversation away from his past, they might be able to come to some sort of understanding on how to navigate their way through co-parenting.

He pressed the white button when it rang again, telegraphing her impatience. "Yeah, sorry. Come on up."

Shannyn stomped up the stairs to his apartment. Jonas didn't have any right to simply make demands where Emma was concerned. He hadn't even asked if they were busy on Saturday. He'd just left that infernal message stating he would be picking them up. She didn't take orders. It was time to set him straight on that.

Jonas held the door open, only his arm visible as she approached from the stairwell. When she came around the corner, everything in her body froze.

He was naked except for a white scrap of cloth that might, in some circles, have passed for a towel. It hung low, delineating the hollows of his hips and leading to tapered abs all the way up to deliciously muscled arms and shoulders.

There was no way she could hide the shock or frank admiration from her face. Jonas Kirkpatrick was physically stunning. Full stop.

"Sorry I took so long. I was in the shower."

"So I see." Shannyn halted in the doorway, avoiding his gaze. Her eyes remained firmly fixed on the center of his chest. The sight of the narrow band of white was arousing at the very least. As she stared at his pecs, he inhaled, and they expanded before her eyes. She had to do something besides gawk like a nitwit!

"Come on in." He finally stood aside, leaving her room to pass by him into the apartment.

Compared to her house, the living arrangements were sparse. The living room held a small drop-leaf table and two chairs, a home gym and a battered sofa in front of a stand holding a thirteen-inch TV/DVD combo. It was meager accommodation, even for a bachelor. She glanced around the corner, seeing doors to what presumably was a bathroom and bedroom, and she'd passed the tiny galley kitchen on the way in. She'd stayed in hotel suites bigger than his apartment.

"It's not very big. But with only me here…" His voice trailed off and he shrugged, making no move to excuse himself to get dressed.

"It's fine." She tried a bland smile. She knew he hadn't missed her initial reaction, from the smug expression on his face. She ignored it and tried to find a place for her gaze to land. She couldn't lose sight of the reason for her visit. He had no right to assume anything.

Jonas adjusted the towel with one hand. Shannyn's nerves were shot and she wasn't sure if it was still the cause of her visit creating such a reaction or the fact that he was standing before her nearly naked. She was struck by a memory—a good one for once—of herself and a hot shower after a particularly nasty walk in the rain when his truck had broken down. They hadn't slept together yet, so he'd let her have the bathroom first, and when he came out later after his shower with his towel wrapped around his hips, one thing had led to another.

His smile seemed to flirt with her, and on top of the potent memory, it wreaked havoc with her intentions.

"How are you, Shan?"

And damned if she didn't blush like a schoolgirl. She inhaled, shoring up her defenses against his unwitting charm. "I'm fine."

"Is Emma okay?"

She spun, again avoiding looking at him. "Emma's fine. How are you?"

"I'm *fine*." He deliberately parroted the word they'd already used several times, and her consternation grew as she realized he was still awfully good at getting around her without even intending it. "Right as rain."

He spread his hands to demonstrate, and the towel slipped. He caught it quickly, revealing nothing beyond the hollow of his hip, but her eyes followed the direction and in that split second she saw the scar, long and angry and jagged, big enough she couldn't possibly miss it.

"Jonas," she whispered, unable to tear her eyes away from the towel that hid his wound once more.

His lips thinned to a hard line, all the earlier teasing wiped clean from his expression. "Stop. I don't want your pity."

She met his gaze evenly. "Of course you don't, and that's not what I meant. But it does look horrible, and I'm sorry for what you went through."

"I'm alive, and there's a hell of a lot more who aren't."

Shannyn paused as his eyes skittered away from hers. Any cockiness he'd exhibited had evaporated. But with his last sentence, things became crystal clear. Survivor's guilt. She didn't know why she hadn't thought of it before. But it all made sense now. He'd been hurt, but he'd gotten out. Who hadn't? And why did he feel so guilty about it?

He turned away, disappearing into a room on the right, she presumed to get dressed. She'd be a liar if she didn't admit to herself that the sight of him nearly naked wasn't an extreme pleasure. She'd been right about what she'd guessed was beneath those lovely T-shirts he was so fond of wearing. Injury or not, his physique was splendid. Her fingers had fairly itched to caress the skin of his ribs.

But that wasn't her place anymore. It was a physical reaction. It had nothing to do with the reality of their situation.

When he returned, he had covered his scar with denim and was buttoning up a light shirt.

"The scar is why you don't wear shorts."

"I don't want questions. Or sympathy. Or revulsion." He finished buttoning his shirt, and his hands dropped to his sides.

"I wondered, when you wore jeans the other night and it so hot."

She put her purse down on the small dining table, wanting to sit but waiting to be invited to do so.

"Meeting Emma was hard enough. I didn't want to have to answer questions about my scar. Although I ended up talking to her about it, anyway."

He stood several feet away, not inviting her to make herself comfortable, and she felt more awkward with each passing moment.

"She had a wonderful time." Shannyn's lips curved a little, a slight invitation to make things more comfortable. Most of her temper had dissipated once she'd seen his scar. "Despite any mishaps. And she enjoyed our lunch out a lot."

"Then why are you here?"

Her smile vanished at his blunt tone, bringing back her motive with distinct clarity. "I think we need to work out a visitation schedule."

"A what?"

Shannyn blinked at his incredulous tone. She'd heard his voice on her answering machine and didn't know what to think. She'd thought that he would come over now and then, spend some time with Emma. But after their first meeting, he'd called with that lunch invitation, and now it was a plan for an air show. She didn't quite know how to feel about that. She wasn't sure Emma was ready for a one-on-one outing with Jonas. Wasn't sure Jonas was ready for that, either. And there was no rhyme or reason to his invitations. It made it awfully difficult to say no.

"Don't you think we should? Set up boundaries, I mean?"

He ran a hand over his cropped hair and shook his head. "You're serious."

Shannyn folded her hands in front of her. "Yes, I am. For one, Emma asks questions like a normal five-year-old. Like when you're coming over again. When she'll see you. What you'll do together. I don't know how to answer her, and that's not fair. It's confusing to her."

"But you must have gotten my message. About this weekend."

Shannyn nodded, wary of rushing the conversation, wanting to make sure she got it right. It was good that Jonas was excited about spending time with Emma, but she couldn't shake the nagging feeling that Jonas was facing his own demons right now and that it would be better if they spent time together with Shannyn around. If they set up boundaries, it would help her as much as it helped Emma. It would be easier if she knew and could prepare, rather than be hit with seeing him out of the blue.

"Yes, of course I got your message. And it was a reminder to me that we should talk this out, decide how we're going to proceed. I think your visitation should have structure."

"You're setting restrictions."

She bit down on her lip. Perhaps she was, but that wasn't exactly how she meant it to be. "I'm not trying to stiff you on time with her, Jonas. It's just…I'm not sure I'm comfortable with your plans for this weekend. I think it should be—"

"Supervised time." He finished the sentence flatly.

She sighed. "Can we sit down and talk about this? All this standing and gawking and I feel like we're going head to head or something."

He motioned towards the single item of furniture—the battered couch—and she sat down, comfortable until he took the cushion farthest away from her.

"Like I said—supervised time." He didn't let go of his point. "Unless you can show me that I can trust you with her."

She held her breath for a moment, expecting him to lose his

cool. Her fingers dug into the edge of the cushions. This wasn't going at all the way she'd hoped.

"You don't trust me. God, Shan. You should know I'd never do anything to hurt Emma." His eyes pinned her, hotly accusing. "Is that really what you think of me?"

Her fingers relaxed slightly, but she wasn't sure how to proceed. It wasn't a matter of trusting him, per se. She knew he'd never do anything to hurt Emma, not intentionally. Some of her doubts had to do with the changes in him, and she knew to broach the topic was to push a hot button.

But she also knew that many of her reservations had to do with herself and how she felt about being near him so often. It had been difficult enough, having Emma as a constant reminder of how much she'd loved him. Now to see him in the flesh on a regular basis—each time cut her a little deeper. It didn't get easier. Quite the opposite. Being with him reminded her both of how she'd felt about him and how little had changed.

"If you were in my shoes, would you let her go so easily? Look at this rationally. I don't doubt your intentions, not at all." She angled herself on the couch, scared to face him yet knowing she must. Knowing she had to say the hard words. "Six years ago you left and never looked back. And now you're here. You've discovered you have a daughter. I don't doubt your motives with regard to Emma. But you hate me for keeping her from you, and you are a different man. You can deny it all you want. But it's true. Something has changed you, and until I understand what and how it will affect Emma, the visits will be supervised."

He got up from the couch. "So what, I get to visit her at your house a few nights a week? What kind of father would that make me?"

"What kind of father do you want to be?"

She'd asked herself that same question all day. His message

hadn't even asked for a reply. He'd just said he would be there Saturday at one o'clock. It had sounded like an order, not an invitation. She'd been tempted to call, but decided talking to him in person would be better.

How *did* he see himself as a father? She'd wondered about it all the while she'd been at work and had gotten his address from his file. What did he want out of his relationship with his daughter? Wondered even as she'd stopped at home to change into her favorite jeans and top, knowing she was going to see him again. Asked it as she'd dropped Emma off for a play date at Lisa's and as she'd stood in the foyer of his apartment building for a full ten minutes before ringing the security buzzer.

What kind of father did Jonas want to be? A part-time one? Full time? She remembered the way he'd looked at her as he'd come across the lawn with Emma's hand in his. Did he want to be a father that sent presents on birthdays and Christmas or one-half of the set that included a wife and mother?

It was the last that caught her every time. Six years ago she might have accepted an offer like that. But she looked at him and could honestly say she didn't think she could trust him not to break her heart all over again. She didn't know how to compete with his career.

"Are you serious? What kind of father do I want to be?" He got up and started to pace, his gait only slightly uneven. "You're asking questions I don't know how to answer. I just go through this day to day, trying to make sense of everything. I'm sorry but my 'big picture' is slightly myopic right now!"

Shannyn took a deep breath, trying not to rise to the bait. "That's what I want to find out. How do you see this playing out? How involved do you want to be in Emma's life?"

He faced her squarely. "I want to be her father and everything that entails."

"It's not all bedtime stories and barbecues. Sometimes it's really hard. So you need to decide what sort of a commitment you can make to her. I don't want to get her hopes up only to have you decide it's too much and back away."

"You think I'd do that?"

"Your commitment record is a little shaky."

"Say what you mean. My commitment record is shaky with *you*."

Heat bloomed in her neck, making its way up to her cheeks. He was right. He'd never had a problem committing to the Army or his unit. He'd run from *her*. She needed to remember that.

"We need to settle this, Jonas."

"Shannyn, there is no 'we.' It's better that way and we both know it." He resumed pacing. "I cannot believe you are honestly sitting there thinking about there being a you and me."

Shannyn felt as though she'd been struck. Whether or not Jonas had been thinking it or not, she had, and it was clear to her now that any atmosphere she'd detected between them earlier, any flirting he'd promoted, had been misinterpreted.

She didn't trust him. She didn't know him. He was a different man but in some ways nothing had changed. For all her intentions today, Jonas was the one making the first real step to setting boundaries. It should have been a relief. Instead she found herself irrationally blinking back tears that she didn't want him to see.

"I'm sorry if that's harsh." His voice gentled slightly. "I just think we have to be honest here. You are still furious with me for not taking you with me. And I'm still angry with you for keeping Emma from me. To start anything between us would be foolish at the very least."

It sounded so perfectly reasonable.

She lifted her chin. She had been thinking it. How could she not, when the only man she'd ever loved was back and had landed smack-dab in her business? He was right about them being angry at each other, but it wasn't quite so easy for her to ignore the feelings she'd always had for him.

"You're right, of course," she responded, as coolly as she could. Somehow she had to get the topic back on track. "Regardless, we have to resolve the visitation issue."

He ran a hand over his head in frustration. "In the Army we just move on and leave the past behind."

She pointed at his leg. "That's a lie and you know it. There's a lot you haven't left behind."

"Let it go."

"I can't. I have to know."

"Know what?"

Her breath strangled her as she tried to straighten her shoulders. All these years she'd wondered, and now she had the opportunity to ask him and fear held her captive. No, she had to ask. She couldn't leave this time without knowing the truth.

"Why you left me without a word. Why *did* you do it, Jonas? You transferred out and never spoke to me again. Just like that. And I was left here with a baby on the way and no one to rely on but myself."

"You think it was easy to leave you?"

She was surprised at how he raised his voice. Somehow this was developing into an argument, but she kept it going because she thought perhaps it was the only way to get to the truth.

"That's exactly what I think. I think that you had your fun with me, but when the call came to go, you were ready. More than ready. I think you thought of nothing more than what was in your sights. Being a sharpshooter."

"You're wrong!"

She stood up, angry now because he'd never said a single word to make her think anything different. "How on earth would I know?"

The words hung in the air between them, crackling with hostility and something darker, something persuasive.

"Because of this."

Before she could breathe, he stepped up to her, gripped her waist with his right hand and pulled her close, pressing his lips to hers.

No warning. No prelude. Just mouth-to-mouth pent-up passion that made her knees turn watery and her heart pound ridiculously.

She wound her arms around his neck, kissing him back as if he were her lifeline.

The kiss gentled, grew fuller as their tongues twined and meshed. When he needed breath, he pulled away and rested his forehead against hers. She opened her eyes, marveling at seeing his lashes against his cheeks.

"Jonas," she whispered.

He pushed her away, stepping back, in control once more.

"You came here for answers, Shan. And I don't have answers. I don't have a plan or a schedule for this. You think I left you without a thought, and that's far from the truth. But you want more of me than I can give. You always have."

"No, I…"

"I'm Emma's father and I won't abandon her. But there's not enough of me for you, too. Don't you understand that?"

"Maybe if you helped me understand…"

"I can't. You'd better go."

Her thoughts, her senses, were all jumbled up and she couldn't make heads or tails of what had just happened. "About Saturday…I'm not comfortable with you taking Emma to the air show on your own. I think it's too soon."

"I never meant to take her by myself. The invitation was for both of you. Although that seems to be a mistake now, considering what just happened."

Shannyn paused, still trying to regain her balance. Maybe if she could get him in another setting. One that was more like the life he was comfortable with. Maybe then he'd open up a little, help her understand.

"It's a simple outing. Let's not make it more complicated than it has to be. If Emma agrees, we'll both go with you."

"If I'm going to build a relationship with her, we need to spend time together."

"I'm sorry if me coming with the package makes it difficult."

He smiled at her but it wasn't warm. "Don't worry about it. It's not my feelings that matter. She'll be more secure with you there with her, too."

Shannyn blinked. Somehow Jonas still had the ability to surprise her. His insight into Emma's feelings, even after their argument, was incredibly thoughtful.

"In the future, it might be good if you *asked* if we were busy or if it's a good time to visit. And I'll do my best to accommodate."

Jonas nodded. "I appreciate it."

"We're both feeling our way, Jonas. Let's just give it time."

"Time," he echoed, going to the door and opening it for her.

She'd had six years of time. Six years of resenting him for leaving and six years of remembering what it was to love him.

Now he was back—possibly for good.

Dealing with that wasn't anything time could cure.

"I'll see you Saturday," she offered weakly, grabbing her purse.

"One o'clock," he reminded her.

When the door shut behind her, she pressed her fingers to her lips. And knew that despite her best intentions, she was leaving with more questions than answers.

# CHAPTER EIGHT

SHE'D forgotten about his physiotherapy appointment. After Jonas had discovered Emma was his, it had seemed pointless to change therapists, and when she'd reminded him briefly about the paperwork not being completed, he'd answered with a terse "never mind." Avoiding each other was no longer an option.

Thursday, when she checked the morning's files, his name was there—"Jonas Kirkpatrick"—and just seeing it sent a little thrill through her. A flutter in her tummy, a smile on her lips.

*Oh no,* she cautioned herself. Remembering the past was one thing, but getting fluttery and silly after a kiss was another matter altogether.

That kiss had been shocking. Not because he'd done it—there was enough chemistry sizzling between them lately it seemed inevitable now that she looked at it in hindsight—but the way the brief contact had affected her threw her for a loop. Her fingers ran possessively over the white label on his file.

She couldn't help but wonder what it had meant. In one breath they'd been arguing. Her words—"How on earth would I know?"—had precipitated it. Did it mean he hadn't been as flippant about leaving as she'd thought? Did he have regrets of his own? Or had it just been the frustration of the moment bubbling over?

She put the file back on the stack of morning appointments, letting her fingers linger over the brown material. His kiss was exactly the same as it had been years before. He tasted the same. The feel of his lips on hers ached with familiarity. She'd tried to dismiss all the signs. Credit the past for the long looks they'd shared or her reaction to his brief touches. Blaming the flutters on simple nostalgia and the fact that they shared a daughter. But actually kissing him again had been a turning point that she couldn't ignore.

Kissing him felt right in a way that nothing had been right since he'd gone away. With one kiss she started longing for things she hadn't let herself long for since Emma had been born.

With one kiss, it had stopped being about what had been between them in the past. And had moved firmly into the territory of what Shannyn wanted for the future.

And what she wanted terrified her. Loving Jonas would be a risk, and she wasn't a risk taker. He was still in the Army. He would still work where they told him to work. And she knew that he would still go, rather than choose her, choose them. She closed the appointment book firmly.

At that same moment the door opened and he walked through it, larger than life in his regular work clothes. His bearing—so straight, so tall and confident—garnered looks of approval.

Then his eyes met hers and she felt it clear to her core. The kiss that had been present in her memory now seemed to tingle on her lips. She could feel the way his fingers had dug into her arms as he pulled her close. The way his breath had fluttered against her cheeks as he pressed his forehead to hers.

He paused longer than necessary, the door handle forgotten in his hand. The longing to cross the room and find his arms again was crazy, but strong. Her breath caught. It wasn't that she hadn't moved on after Jonas. It wasn't that being a single mom made it hard to date, even though that's how she'd explained it for years.

Suddenly seeing him again, for the first time since they'd kissed, she realized that what she'd done all these years was waited. She'd been waiting for him.

And now here he was, a little older and with a lot more baggage, unwilling to let her in. And she was unwilling to ask him to.

Jonas must have realized how they were staring because he finally let the door handle go. It took its lazy time shutting behind him. He approached the desk, his eyes only leaving Shannyn's briefly as he gave his name to the receptionist.

Shannyn stepped forward. "Hello, Jonas." The words seemed strangled and forced. Yet to say more, here in public, seemed too intimate, inappropriate.

"Shan."

She swallowed at the warm tone of the single syllable. Was she just imagining it? Or did he seem less aloof now than he had before?

"I forgot about your appointment today."

"I didn't."

He put one hand in his pocket and balanced his weight on his good hip. Had he thought about that kiss as much as she had?

They had to stop staring at each other.

"I told Emma about Saturday. She's very excited."

His lips tipped up and her heart did a slow turnover. Simply knowing that he'd pleased their daughter made him smile and his eyes light, and that touched her.

"I'm excited, too. I've got to be on base in the morning, otherwise I could have taken you both to the static display."

"Don't worry." She dipped her head, suddenly shy. "We're both looking forward to the afternoon."

His eyebrows came together a bit, and she licked her lips nervously.

"Me, too," was his simple reply. His forehead relaxed and she thought for a moment he was going to come toward her.

She turned her head slightly at the sound of a door opening. "It looks like Geneva is ready for you now."

He turned toward the door leading to the treatment area.

"Jonas?"

He stopped, turning only his head to look at her.

The words stuck in her throat. "Nothing, never mind," she muttered. "I'll see you when you're done."

He was gone several minutes when curiosity got the better of her. She rarely interrupted a therapy session, but today she wanted to see—to really see—what had happened to his leg. More than an accidental glimpse of the angry scar marring the skin of his thigh. He had been so self-conscious about it the other day. And she knew if she were to ask to see it, he'd find an excuse.

She knocked on the door to the exercise room. Inside she saw Jonas on a blue mat on the floor, Geneva kneeling beside him, her touch gentle on his leg as he bent at the waist, stretching the stiff muscles.

"Hi," she offered quietly.

Jonas looked up. "Shannyn."

He was wearing gray shorts, the line of his incision clear and imprecise. His eyes darted away from hers, the twist of his mouth communicating his consternation. She probably wasn't playing fair. He couldn't hide his injury from her here.

But he needed to know she accepted him with it, so she stepped into the room and moved ahead to a bench a few feet away.

"We're just finishing up," Geneva explained, smiling at Shannyn. By now the staff all pretty much knew that Jonas was Emma's father; it was difficult to keep very much a secret in such a small group. "You want some privacy?"

Jonas colored while Shannyn smiled, shaking her head. "No, that's okay. I just wanted to see how he was making out."

She turned her attention fully to Jonas. He lengthened out his leg, his foot nearly reaching the end of the mat. "Soooo." She drew the word out. "How are you?"

"Not bad, besides having a gimp leg," he grumbled.

"You're hardly limping anymore."

"That's right," Geneva added. "Your range of motion and strength are really coming along."

He finished stretching out his quadriceps, and Shannyn heard the small gasp as he reached the point where he could go no further. When Geneva let him relax the pose, she got to her feet. "Good work today, Jonas. I'll see you next week. Don't forget to work on those stretches every day."

She left, leaving Jonas on the mat and Shannyn on the bench beside him.

"Why are you here?" He folded his legs, partially covering the scar with his arm.

"Because here it's harder for you to hide. You reveal all to your PT but the moment I catch a glimpse of your leg, you run and cover up. I wanted to see it."

His lips thinned. "Why? It's just a scar."

Shannyn tucked her hair behind her ears, then shook her head in disagreement. "It's more than a scar. It's more than a physical injury, Jonas, and you know it."

"But it's my problem, not yours."

"What if I said I wanted to help you?"

He'd been avoiding her gentle gaze, but now he faced her head-on, frustration a dark spark in his eyes. "I'd say you're crazy."

Shannyn slid off the bench and onto her knees on the mat. Maybe she was crazy. But now they were bound by the link of their daughter. Her lingering feelings for him meant that when he was hurting, she was, too, even if she didn't understand exactly why. His kiss said he wasn't immune to her, either.

"We have a past, Jonas. And now we have a daughter. That ties

# Get FREE BOOKS and FREE GIFTS when you play the...

## LAS VEGAS GAME

*Just scratch off the gold box with a coin. Then check below to see the gifts you get!*

**YES!** I have scratched off the gold box. Please send me my **2 FREE BOOKS** and **2 FREE GIFTS** for which I qualify. I understand that I am under no obligation to purchase any books as explained on the back of this card.

**316 HDL ENWT**          **116 HDL ENW5**

| | |
|---|---|
| FIRST NAME | LAST NAME |

ADDRESS

| | |
|---|---|
| APT.# | CITY |

| | |
|---|---|
| STATE/PROV. | ZIP/POSTAL CODE |

(H-R-03/08)

| 7 | 7 | 7 | Worth TWO FREE BOOKS plus TWO FREE GIFTS! |
| 🍒 | 🍒 | 🍒 | Worth TWO FREE BOOKS! |
| 🔔 | 🔔 | ♣ | TRY AGAIN! |

www.eHarlequin.com

Offer limited to one per household and not valid to current subscribers of Harlequin Romance®. All orders subject to approval.

**Your Privacy -** Harlequin Books is committed to protecting your privacy. Our privacy policy is available online at www.eHarlequin.com or upon request from the Harlequin Reader Service. From time to time we make our lists of customers available to reputable third parties who may have a product or service of interest to you. If you would prefer for us not to share your name and address, please check here.☐

us, don't you see?" She looked straight into his eyes. "We may not be together anymore, but I still care about what happens to you."

Her heart pounded as she put a cool hand on his knee. "Let me help you."

Verbally she'd denied their attraction, but the touch of her fingers on his skin belied the message. With her index finger she gently traced the incision line, noticing how the skin felt different there, thrilling as the muscle beneath her finger contracted at her touch. "I want to help you."

"What if I don't want you to?"

She stopped her finger and let her palm fall. She realized that the scar was longer than the length of her hand. The fact that he could do as much as he could now was a miracle.

"Are you saying you *don't* want me to?"

She leaned forward, moving closer to him. He was balanced on his palms, but when he lifted his right hand, the balance shifted, pushing him closer to her. His fingers reached behind her ear, pulling the hair taut and cupping her neck.

"What if I wanted to kiss you and that's all?"

Her pounding heart shifted into overdrive. The idea was seductive even as she realized by saying it he was refusing to let her in for more than a kiss. Still…if kissing him could break down barriers…help her understand…

She didn't wait but leaned the rest of the way and touched his mouth with hers.

He pushed further forward, taking his other hand off the mat and sliding it behind her other ear, forming a perfect cradle for her head as he opened his mouth, letting her in.

It was sweet perfection, better than the one in his living room. That kiss had been fast, new and fueled by anger and frustration. This time they were both going into it knowing what was coming, and it showed. No rushing, but a willing coming together, soft and accepting. Soon her knees ached and she leaned slightly, curling into his lap while his hands adjusted her head to the right fit.

And still the kiss went on.

He moaned into her mouth, the sound vibrating through her like a string that had been plucked. Her arms curled around his neck and her weight shifted.

He stiffened, going perfectly still before letting her go and resting back on his hands again.

His eyes closed, his mouth no longer soft with passion but tight with pain.

"Oh, Jonas, I'm so sorry," Shannyn gasped, sliding off his lap and kneeling beside him. "I didn't mean to hurt you."

"It's okay."

"What can I do to help?"

"You've done enough."

She recoiled as if slapped, sliding backward and sitting back up on the bench.

Jonas pushed away and got up, less than graceful after the bump to his injury.

"I need to get changed."

Sitting on the low bench, his scar was nearly at Shannyn's eye level. She dragged her eyes away and looked up at him. "Why does it sound like you're blaming me?"

"Maybe I am." He started to walk away.

"We need to talk about this."

"You're awfully fond of talking." His words came back to her as he kept going toward the door.

She ignored his bitter tone. "We can't just leave things this way, Jonas."

He stopped, didn't turn around, but she saw his shoulders rise and fall in a frustrated sigh. They both knew that avoiding each other wouldn't work. They had to clear the air.

"A cup of coffee. That's all I have time for this morning."

A cup of coffee would do if that's all he'd give. At least it would get them out of the office and somewhere neutral. So much of their time lately had been on his turf or hers.

"Sold. I'll meet you out in reception when you're ready."

When he came out minutes later, she grabbed her purse and hustled from behind her desk. She didn't trust him not to leave without waiting for her.

"There's a Timmy's around the corner," he said as they emerged on to the sidewalk. He thumbed in the general direction of a popular coffee chain.

But it would be too easy to get a coffee there and go their separate ways, and Shannyn wanted to hold on to him a little bit longer.

"There's a place I know on Queen that makes great iced cappuccino."

He paused, looking again at the familiar coffee shop and back at her.

"All right."

Jonas followed along, this once. Kissing her had been a mistake, he realized. Both times. The first time he'd been angry and frustrated and remembering all too clearly what it had been like to leave her at the end of that summer. And this morning…this morning had been madness. He knew what folly it was to kiss her again and he'd gone ahead and done it anyway. Slid his hands into that soft hair and pulled her close.

He knew better. He should be putting more distance between them, not kissing her. No matter how he felt about her, the one thing he was sure of was that this would all end badly. It would be better for everyone to stop it all right now. She knew it too, and he was angry with her for putting him in such a position.

She'd initiated the contact, the kiss. And now he was going to have to put a stop to this sort of thing ever happening again.

She stopped before a coffee shop and opened the door, her hair swinging in the breeze as she looked over her shoulder. "You coming?"

He followed her inside and looked around. It certainly wasn't his normal type of establishment. Trendy decor, drinks with long, nearly unpronounceable names. It looked to be a place more suited to poetry readings than a quick cup of joe.

"Jonas? Aren't you going to order?"

He stepped up to the counter, looked at the woman in the plain apron and dared, "Large coffee. Black."

A minute later they picked up their drinks, and Shannyn led them to a table in the corner.

"This wasn't what I had in mind when I said a quick cup of coffee."

She smiled at him but it seemed frail around the edges. "I know."

Not knowing how to respond to that, he took a sip from his cup. For all that the atmosphere wasn't his style, they did know how to brew a good cup of coffee. Shannyn dropped her eyes and sipped on her iced drink, then made circles with her straw.

"Jonas, I wanted to talk because…because something is obviously happening between us and we owe it to Emma to make sure there's as little confusion as possible."

Her logic made sense, but he saw through it. She looked a little too earnest, too innocent. He never should have kissed her the other day. It had sent the wrong message and he'd been foolish to act so impulsively. She wanted more. He could sense it.

"This isn't about pinning me down to some sort of expectation, then."

She had the grace to look uncomfortable. She shifted in her seat and looked down at her cup again.

"Shan, I told you the other day. You want answers and I don't have them. Kissing you was a mistake." He folded his hands on the table before him. "Both times. Because there can't be anything between us."

"But there is something between us. Emma." Shannyn leaned forward, imploring.

"And I want to do the right thing by her, and be a good father. But you and me…it wouldn't work. I hurt you badly when I left. And you destroyed my faith in you when you lied to me. We can't pretend that doesn't exist."

Jonas had to look away after he said it. He wasn't good at lying to her face. Whether or not there should be more to their relationship was irrelevant. There already was. The kisses proved it.

She studied her straw for a few moments. "I knew you were going to say that."

How could he make her understand without telling her more than he should? There was so much inside of him, and it was all so jumbled together that to even attempt anything would be like trying to untangle a ball of string. One complication would get sorted and another knot would present itself. How could he put them all through it?

He knew the things he'd done, the regrets he had. There was no way he wanted to put those on Shannyn or Emma. Even if Shannyn didn't understand it, he knew it was the right thing.

"You have to understand, I'm not the same person I was then. I'm…I've seen and done a lot of things over the years. Things that mean I'll never be the same. It wouldn't be fair to you to bring all that to the table in addition to everything else."

She looked up at him, sipping her drink. He wished she'd say something so he could rid himself of the feeling that he was hanging himself. But she stayed quiet, forcing him to keep talking to avoid empty silence.

"And what would happen if we took things further and then it all fell apart? Who's the real casualty going to be then? Emma."

He felt momentarily guilty for that statement. Shannyn had used Emma's existence as protection only moments before and now he was doing the same thing. The truth of the matter was that he knew *he'd* end up hurt. Worse, he would hurt Shannyn again and that was the last thing he wanted. It had hurt badly enough the first time.

"I think it would be better for everyone if we were just friends."

He was finished. To his mind there was nothing more to say.

She pushed the drink aside, studied her fingers for a few seconds before looking up. She was so beautiful. Gazing into her youthful, hopeful face he felt old and world-weary. He could see what she wanted, even if she denied it to herself. She wanted the fairy tale. The happily-ever-after. And he was the last person on earth to give it to her.

Fairy tales were just that. Tales. They didn't exist. They were there to give false hope in a world that was darker than even she realized.

"What about the kisses?" Her voice ached with sweetness and he wished things were different. That he could just forget it all and love her like she wanted.

"An echo from the past, that's all."

It had the desired effect: her eyes dropped and her shoulders relaxed.

He should let it end there, but he hated knowing he'd hurt her in any way.

"I still want you to come to the air show on Saturday. We're still going to parent Emma, and I meant what I said. We should be friends."

"Friends would be the mature thing to do," she agreed, but the light had gone out of her eyes.

It was better now, he reasoned. A small disappointment now versus a big one later.

"I need to get back to the base."

"I need to get back to work, too. I've probably taken too much time as it is."

Shannyn picked up her cup. The mocha-flavored mixture had lost its appeal. She'd obviously misread his signals from before. Foolishly she'd let herself hope that maybe she still meant something to him. This morning his touch had been so tender, so gentle. And fantasy had gotten the best of her and she'd allowed herself to picture the three of them—herself, Jonas, Emma—all together, happy and strong.

What she'd done was let herself be foolish and forget all the reasons why she and Jonas wouldn't work. He was right. She still resented him for leaving, and despite moments of accord, she knew he couldn't put aside the fact that she'd kept Emma hidden from him.

Apparently he hadn't had the same vision of familial bliss. She wasn't surprised. He hadn't wanted those things before, either. It wasn't his fault she'd let silly fancy sweep her away after a few kisses. She needed to do what she'd always done. Make sure Emma was safe, secure and happy.

If being friends with Jonas was the way to do that, she'd do it. Even if it killed her.

They were outside in the glaring brilliance of late morning when a call interrupted their steps.

"Sgt. Kirkpatrick!"

Jonas and Shannyn turned as a fresh-faced young man jogged up. Like Jonas, he was dressed in ordinary combats, only two stripes on his sleeve instead of the three that Jonas sported.

"Good morning, Corporal." Jonas smiled.

"I'm glad I ran into you." The young soldier grinned. "I'm sorting a few things before I leave tomorrow."

"You're shipping out?" Shannyn interjected.

He looked at her, the smile never leaving his face. "Yes ma'am. Sgt. Kirkpatrick was my instructor. I'm headed for Base Petawawa in the morning."

"I see."

"Good luck to you, Cpl. Benner." Jonas held out his hand. "Give 'em hell."

"Count on it."

Shannyn realized that the effusive youth before her was a man ready to do a man's job, with an infectious enthusiasm she recalled seeing on Jonas's face that same summer he'd gone to Edmonton. When she looked up at Jonas, she was surprised to see a mixture of pride, enthusiasm and longing beaming from his features.

He hadn't changed. Not that much.

"You look like you wish you could go with him," she teased.

The men broke hands and Jonas looked down at her. "Maybe I do…but those days seem to be over."

"Oh, I don't know," Corporal Benner joked. "I saw you running on the course the other day, and the leg's looking great." The young man turned his attention to Shannyn. "Sgt. Kirkpatrick is something of a hero on base, ma'am. Best shot in the country, if the rumors are true."

"Benner," Jonas started to protest.

"Not many men do what he's done and live to tell about it, ma'am, and that's the truth. It's too bad he's not still out in the field. We all count ourselves the luckiest bast…fellas in the Army to have him as a teacher."

"Cpl. Benner," Jonas said more firmly.

"Sorry, Sarge." Benner looked a little sheepish, but not enough to resist throwing Shannyn a wink. "But it's true."

He held out his hand to Jonas again. "I've got to get going, but thanks again, Sgt. Kirkpatrick."

"Good luck, Benner."

"Thanks. Ma'am." He nodded at Shannyn before jogging away.

"He's had his caffeine this morning," Shannyn laughed lightly. She was still reeling from all that the young soldier had said. Jonas was a hero. He'd done great things. Things he refused to talk about.

"He's young, and full of the belief he can make the world a better place," Jonas responded, his face clouding. "Give him a few weeks in combat and that'll all change."

"Like it did for you?"

He didn't answer. They resumed their steps, walking back to the clinic.

"Jonas? Are you really a hero?"

He snorted, a humorless chuckle of irony. "Hardly."

"Then why would Cpl. Benner say it?"

He wouldn't look at her. "I have no idea."

He was hiding something, but she didn't know what. She wondered what he might have done that constituted hero status.

She tried a different tack. "Are you really the best shot in the Army?"

He kept walking, his gait even and steady. "There's an official sniping record in place. My name ain't on it."

"But unofficially?"

He angled his head in her direction, a wry smile cracking his stony expression at her tenacity and insight. "Unofficially is another story."

She couldn't stop the beam of pride that shot through her at his admission. It was what he'd wanted, when he'd been younger and idealistic like Benner. It made her proud to know he'd accomplished his goal.

"And you really did run the other day?"

"Yeah."

They were back at the parking lot, and their steps slowed as they reached his truck.

"Thanks for the coffee," she said.

"You're welcome. I'm...I'm glad we got things straightened out. I think it'll be better for everyone if we keep things clear. If we keep things friendly between us. Consistent for Emma."

He wanted to be friends.

Shannyn looked up into his eyes, wishing he'd look at her again the way he had once. Free of shutters and caution. Hungry to drink in the sight of her face the same way she was his. She was more certain than ever that Jonas had done great things, even if he refused to talk about it. Every day, as his recovery progressed, she sensed a greater strength in him. It was hard not to be attracted to that. Even harder to resist a man who was concerned about her daughter. It was all she'd ever wanted. It was hard to hate him for pushing her aside, when it was clearly to Emma's benefit.

"We're still good for Saturday?"

"We're good." He smiled. "Tell Emma I'm looking forward to it."

"I will."

Their gazes clung for a few seconds and her heart lifted. Because no matter what came out of his mouth, his eyes said there was something more.

He climbed into the truck and started the engine. As she watched him drive away, she wished she weren't looking forward to it quite so much.

# CHAPTER NINE

WHEN Shannyn answered the doorbell, Jonas was surprised to see that both she and Emma were dressed in red and white.

Shannyn's hair was plaited in an intricate braid, revealing the pale curve of her neck. For a brief second, he remembered how she'd felt in his arms just a few days ago. Her long legs extended beneath the hem of her shorts and ended with cute white tennis shoes. Legs that had been folded up into his lap as she'd pressed her chest to his. He longed to run his fingers over the smooth length of them.

This was ridiculous. He was here for an outing, nothing more. He'd made it perfectly clear during their coffee date that more wasn't possible. No matter what he truly felt. Protecting her was more important than his attraction.

"I didn't realize you'd take the festivities quite this seriously," he joked, looking down at Emma. Despite their similar dress of white shorts and red T-shirts, he realized again how much Emma resembled him, and it filled him with paternal joy. He remembered seeing pictures of himself as a small boy. The eyes, the curls, the shape of the lips…there was no doubt Emma was his daughter, and he felt a shaft of pride knowing it.

"It's Canada Day. If ever there were a day to be patriotic…"

"Then it's today," he agreed. Being in the forces, much of his identity and pride was wrapped up in his nationality. It was more than a long weekend to him. Spending it with Shannyn was probably not the smartest move, but he was determined to enjoy this one last indulgence. Soon she'd see that Emma could spend time with him alone, and these family scenes would come to an end. It would be the smart thing to do.

"You look great. I didn't realize you'd dress up, so I brought something for you to put on before we go." He held out a small bag, handed it to Emma. She reached inside and pulled out a flat package covered in plastic.

"Tattoos!"

He smiled. He hadn't been able to resist the temporary, maple leaf tattoos at the store where he'd stopped for snacks on his way to the house.

"Should we put them on?"

"Mama?"

Jonas smiled at the indulgent way Shannyn looked at Emma. When she turned her warm gaze back to him, his grin broadened. It would be a different sort of Canada Day than they'd spent together before, but he was no less happy with it. Maybe there wouldn't be swimming followed by fireworks on a blanket…but he could see she hadn't lost her sense of fun. He had worried about there being tension between them today. So much had happened since his last visit with Emma. Perhaps Shannyn had taken his plea to heart to stay friends for Emma's sake.

Shannyn held open the door. "Why not. Come on in."

Emma went first, choosing to have her maple leaf emblazoned on her cheek. "Very cool," Jonas complimented. Emma spun to rush to the bathroom and check the mirror. When Jonas looked back, Shannyn was waiting for him with tattoo and sponge at the ready.

"Where do you want it?"

He met her eyes. The kitchen was strangely quiet without Emma's vivacity. "On my cheek, too, I guess. I didn't have time to change after working this morning, so it won't be visible anywhere else."

Shannyn took one from the packet that was shaped like a rippling flag. Suddenly his combat jacket seemed tight, constricting. When her cool fingers touched his skin he held his breath. She was so gentle. Standing so close, the tip of her tongue between her teeth as she concentrated, rubbing the temporary sticker with the damp sponge.

He wondered what it would be like to kiss her again. *Stop thinking about it, you fool,* he fretted to himself. Two kisses had been more than enough to tell him he was in dangerous territory. He'd been the one to put on the brakes, and he'd do well to remember it. It had been the right decision. No matter how she made him feel, he knew it was better all around this way. He wasn't capable of more. There could be no kisses or meaningful touches.

Before he could think about it further, she stepped away. "There you go. All done."

Shannyn put the sponge down on the counter. What had started out as a fun game had suddenly changed. As soon as she'd touched the smooth skin of his cheek, she'd been reminded of the way he'd kissed her at his apartment. Without prelude, without apology. Like the years between them hadn't happened. The way he'd cupped her neck and she'd crawled into his lap on Thursday.

"What about you?" he asked hoarsely.

She swallowed. The last thing she needed right now was him touching her, in any way. She took the last tattoo and pressed it against her arm. "I can do my own. Why don't you take Emma out and buckle her in?"

"Shannyn, I…"

She looked up from her arm, holding the paper against the skin. "I know. I get it. Friends, Jonas."

He paused, his eyes unsure. Shannyn made herself hold her ground. It was tempting to want to know what he'd meant to say, but the boundaries had been set, and the more she thought about it, the more she realized it was the right approach.

"I'm glad you're coming," he finished, looking away.

She was glad, too. Too glad. At first, seeing him had been a shock, then a complication she didn't want. And then something had changed. She'd stopped resenting him quite so much. Had started thinking of him while she lay in bed at night.

But now there was Emma to consider, and Shannyn had been hurt badly enough that there was some comfort in being friends. It was safer. It was still complicated, maybe even more than it had been in the beginning. But it was because the more she saw him the more she was reminded of how much there had been between them. How much there still *was* between them. She'd promised herself she'd be strong. It was proving more difficult with each day. She had such a weakness for him. Nothing had changed for her, except now she was unwilling to risk her heart. She'd jumped in recklessly the first time and it was a lesson well learned. She'd tested those waters the other day over coffee, and it had reinforced her knowledge that she couldn't go through a full-fledged breakup with him again. Not ever.

Nothing had changed for Jonas, either, and that was the sticking point. He hadn't cared enough to make a life with her before, and he'd made it clear on Thursday that he still didn't. Only as Emma's parents, and that was the sum of their relationship.

But it didn't stop her from caring, not when he looked at her the way he was looking at her right now.

"I'll be right out," she whispered, not trusting herself to say more.

Jonas took Emma to the truck. When Shannyn joined them

a few minutes later, she couldn't help but smile at Emma's chatter. She threw out questions at a mile a minute. Where were they going to watch from? What sorts of planes would there be? Would it be noisy? Had he flown in any of them? Jonas happily answered all her questions, and Shannyn listened to his answers, with Emma sandwiched snugly between them.

Emma's nonstop talking kept the truck from being too quiet and within a few minutes they had crossed the bridge and found parking on the north side of the river.

"I thought the crowd would be smaller on this side," he explained, reaching behind the bench seat for an army blanket and the grocery bag of snacks.

"This is fine," Shannyn answered, and they made their way to an empty space on the grass.

Jonas spread the blanket, and Shannyn felt strangely as if they were on a regular family outing. It didn't matter that their family wasn't a "normal" family unit. Looking around, the scene was much the same. Parents out with children, spreading blankets and handing out water bottles and juice boxes. Others sat in couples, but all waited to see the aircraft fly one by one up the river's path. Some would perform stunts; others would simply showcase their aeronautical abilities and impressive structures. Sitting down on the blanket, she watched Jonas strip his jacket. He leaned back on his arms and soaked up the summer sun.

"You look rested," Shannyn commented, assuming a similar pose.

"I feel rested. Better than I have in a long time."

"Mama! There's a hot dog cart." Emma bounded over and tugged on Shannyn's finger. "Can I get one?"

Jonas sat back up and reached into his jacket for keys. "I can't believe I forgot. I brought a bag of food and left it in the truck."

Shannyn put a hand on his arm. "You stay and enjoy the sun. Emma and I will go." She took the keys from his hand.

He watched them go with a smile. Looking across the green, his eyes fell on a young couple. The man was in combats, like Jonas. He had blond hair and an easy way about him that reminded him of Chris Parker.

The muscles in Jonas's shoulders tightened. He was torn, being here with Shannyn and their daughter, enjoying a summer's afternoon. He wanted it both ways. He kept insisting there could be nothing between them, but at the first opportunity he was with her enjoying her company. He listened to the birds in the elms and maples, his eyes staring up into the cloudless blue sky. What really wasn't fair was that Parker wouldn't ever feel the sun on his face again. And yet Jonas was here. Free. Healthy. With a family he never knew he had. It didn't seem right to him.

Didn't seem right without his best friend.

*Dust. Everywhere, on his skin, in his hair, in his mouth.*

*"I've got him at the door." Chris's hushed murmur came from beside him.*

*"I've got him, Park."*

*"You're clear. Take the shot."*

*The midafternoon sun was unrelenting and he blinked against a bead of sweat that trickled into his eye.*

*He squeezed the trigger, heard the echo of the shot. Seconds later he saw the body fall through his scope.*

*"Damn," Parker murmured, still keeping his voice low. "Over twenty-six hundred. How's it feel to hold the new record?"*

*Jonas angled a wry look over his shoulder. "It feels classified."*

*He laughed quietly and they slid back down the embankment, efficiently folding their gear and packing it.*

*"Good job today. Make sure you've got your canteen. We've got five miles to hike before we're picked up, and we're already behind."*

*Two hours later they were back with the company they'd been assigned to. And thirty minutes after that they were all heading back to the airfield where they'd meet up with the platoon.*

"Daddy. We got the bag."

Jonas came out of the memory with a start and struggled to appear normal. Normal. That was a joke.

Shannyn reached the blanket, and he knew he hadn't covered up his lapse completely because her expression clearly said she knew something was up.

"Emma, why don't you go look at the ducks for a moment while I talk to Jonas. We'll have a snack soon."

Emma went closer to the bank, creeping up on the ducks and gulls that were in the grass. Her giggles reached Jonas's ears and he took long breaths, forcing himself to relax.

"You okay?"

"Yeah." She didn't need to know what he'd been remembering. Besides, it was over now. And this time the memory had been shorter, and he'd snapped back quickly. Maybe it was getting better after all.

"Your leg's all right?"

"Seriously, Shan. I'm fine. I'm just glad to be here."

She took her place back on the blanket, stretching out her legs and drinking in the summer sun. "Your physiotherapy is helping. I noticed at your appointment, and watching you walk today."

Jonas squinted through the sun to look at her, her blond hair gleaming, her slim legs crossed at the ankles. She'd painted her toenails a patriotic red. It helped to rid himself of the memory of Chris Parker. "Emma is helping more."

Just as he said it, Emma plopped down on the blanket next to his knee. "I'm thirsty."

Jonas slapped his leg, ridding himself of the glumness. "By George, so am I. I wonder what's in this bag anyway."

He handed Emma the bag and let her root through it. "Mama! There's lemonade! The pink kind!"

He grinned as Emma pulled out a bottle. "We'd better open it before it gets warm."

Shannyn watched the two of them with a lump in her throat. His fingers unscrewed the cap on the bottle before handing it to Emma and then ruffling her hair. Jonas frightened her on so many levels, but seeing how he responded to Emma touched her deeply. He'd come back and had started making demands, never asking, always expecting his orders to be followed. He'd been cold and autocratic. She supposed his training had taught him that. And naturally she balked at being told what to do. She'd been doing the parent thing single-handedly for years.

Emma reached into the bag and pulled out a paper-wrapped package before plunking herself back on Jonas's lap.

Jonas's penchant for bossiness wasn't what scared her. What scared her most were moments like these. Normal family moments. Moments she deeply wanted for Emma, but ones that were dangerous for her. She couldn't let fancy get the best of her. Like now, when his low laugh reached her ears. The way the muscles corded when Emma tripped and he caught her in his arms. Remembering those arms wrapped around her.

"Shan?"

Jonas held out his hand to her, even that simple gesture tying them together. "I brought sandwiches."

"You mean, you brought a picnic," she teased, but her smile was weak. Jonas had thought of everything, it seemed. It pleased her but threw her off her stride. Usually she was the one looking after details like snacks and blankets.

"I came prepared." He flashed a grin at her.

His grin was like a bolt of lightning, reaching into her and bringing her to life. It made it seem like Jonas had never been away. Even though she knew that being friends was absolutely the right thing to do, she also recognized that it wouldn't take much for her heart to be completely lost all over again. And that terrified her. There were still so many questions between them that were unanswered. Answers she wanted to share with him but that he was unwilling to give. And a niggling fear that if she knew the truth, maybe he was right. Maybe she wouldn't look at him in the same way.

He still held out the sandwich and wiggled his eyebrows at her. In all the times she'd seen him since he'd returned, never had he been this mellow, this approachable. Maybe he was feeling as comfortable in their new "friend" capacity as she was uncomfortable. She took the paper packet from his hand and unwrapped it. "You sure did."

For minutes they munched quietly. Emma sat in the vee of Jonas's outstretched legs, her head leaning back against his chest. He lifted one arm and pointed out over the river at a duck taking off; Emma raised a finger and followed the same path. When Emma's glowing face turned to say something, he leaned forward and kissed her forehead as laughter shook his chest.

There was no denying it now. He was a part of Emma's life and by extension, hers, too. And somehow she would have to find a way to fortify her heart against him. Keep the status quo. Make sure nobody got hurt. Establish themselves as friends, the way he wanted. For Shannyn the way to her heart had never been with pretty speeches or flowers or any of the traditional trappings. She found that seeing him with Emma, seeing how he naturally responded to her, touched her in a profound way.

But he didn't love her. Perhaps he never had. So she'd have to bury her own emotions if it came to that.

The very thought seemed laughable. She could never be just friends with Jonas. Feelings would always get in the way.

The loudspeaker crackled and an unseen emcee's voice echoed over the riverbank.

Shannyn watched the show quietly, absorbing the way Jonas put his arm around Emma to point out features of the different aircraft. There were small biplanes and single-engine private craft. A pair of old WWII bombers flew up the river in formation, their engines rumbling loudly. Jonas laughed when Emma put her hands over her ears as the CF-18s did a fly-by and when she laughed at the painted nose of the A-10 as it screamed past.

"Do you know what they call that?" he asked her.

She shook her head and he grinned. "A warthog."

She giggled. Shannyn caught his eye. "She's having a wonderful time."

"So am I." His gaze held hers, making the simple words mean more.

"Me, too," Shannyn replied, and meant it. She was glad she'd come along, although from the way Jonas and Emma were getting along, she needn't have worried about them spending time alone. She'd never seen him so relaxed, and it was clear Emma trusted him completely.

The river quieted as the announcer told everyone to listen. An aircraft was approaching. Still, there was no sound. Jonas's smile grew with each passing second. He nodded to Shannyn, then pointed at a speck behind them in the distance. It took her a few seconds to find it, but his trained eye had picked it up right away.

Still there was no sound, until suddenly the plane passed in front of them and the boom followed. Jonas's voice echoed the announcer—"That's a B1B stealth bomber."

When the words were out of his mouth, his face clouded over. His jaw tensed slightly and his eyes lost all their warmth. Shannyn could tell he was remembering something. She wished he'd tell her what. What was so painful that the memory kept haunting him over and over? What was it he couldn't get past?

After the bomber, they looked up high and saw a parachute team jump. Emma's finger pointed and her mouth made an O as the jumpers got closer and closer, their chutes billowing in the wind as they steered themselves toward the ground. Shannyn looked away from the parachute team and examined Jonas instead. Something was wrong. Emma was talking to him, but his face looked as if it had been carved in stone. His eyes, clear green, focused on nothing in particular and his chest barely rose and fell as he breathed. He was pulling away again but this time something was different, and Shannyn couldn't put her finger on it.

One by one the parachutes landed in a wide circle that had been marked off, and the audience clapped enthusiastically. The speaker started again, remarking on the team's accuracy and telling the crowd to look downriver. As the team divested themselves of their chutes, a helicopter wound its way up and toward the wide white-marked circumference—waiting to extract the team.

As the announcer droned on about the challenges of a quick extraction in a combat situation, Shannyn never took her eyes off Jonas. Her heart pounded as his face paled and his hands started to visibly shake. In a matter of a few seconds, he'd gone from vibrant father to a marble statue.

"Emma," she said quietly, tugging on the little girl's sleeve. "Emma, come sit with Mama for a moment."

At Shannyn's quiet, commanding tone, Emma did what she was told. Shannyn put Emma by her right hip, so that she was between Emma and Jonas. The helicopter came closer, closer, the syncopated rhythm filling her ears while Jonas remained deathly calm.

One by one the parachute team was loaded into the waiting helicopter, the end of the performance. But Shannyn felt real fear when she saw a single tear trickle down Jonas's pale cheek. His eyes never blinked, his lips never moved, but that one tear crawled its way down his cheek and dropped off his jaw.

# CHAPTER TEN

NOTHING existed beyond the sound.

Heavy rotor blades cut through the air as the Chinook hovered a few feet from the ground. Jonas could see the pilot, the helicopter close enough that he could see the headset over his ears and his lips moving as he spoke into the mike, the deafening noise of the helo drowning out the nearby voices.

"Let's clear these men out!" The announcer crowed with enthusiasm.

*"Let's clear out, eh, Parker? Or that fiancée of yours'll get bored and find someone else," Jonas teased his partner as they bounced along the dirt road.*

*"Yeah, well it sure won't be you," Parker shot back with a wide grin.*

*Jonas laughed.*

*The Iltis hit a rut, jostling the soldiers sitting in the back. "Hey, Sgt. Kirkpatrick. There's something up ahead."*

*Jonas leaned forward, peering through the windshield of the Iltis. Before he could open his mouth, everything shifted. He felt himself thrown into the air, out of the back of the vehicle. For a moment he was weightless. And everything went black.*

*At first he was only aware of sounds. Shouts and skids as the rest of the vehicles in their small convoy ground to a halt behind them. Then it was smells.*

*The heavy, coppery scent of blood mingled with dust filled his nostrils in the desert heat, but he saw nothing. Sudden weakness caused his eyes to close against the blinding sun. Gunfire echoed, tinny and thin, along with the dry crackle of fire—the charred, mangled pieces of the Iltis.*

*Everything was fuzzy, like being underwater.*

*With huge effort, Jonas turned his head to the left, opening his eyes enough to squint. What he saw was a narrow radius of carnage. Parker was dead, his mangled form sprawled motionless on the hard gravel of the road. Jonas blindly touched his leg, drawing his shaking fingers up and seeing the blood staining the tips as he fought the nausea curling through his stomach. Behind him he heard the shouts of his comrades; rifle fire popping over the ridge.*

*He heard a shout for a medic. He heard someone calling to get on the radio for an extraction. His eyes slid closed, trying to keep things linear and logical in his mind. Confused shouts echoed all around him.*

*"Hold on, Sarge." A steady voice was at his right side, but he couldn't distinguish who it was. Hands pressed against his leg and he gritted his teeth. "Help's coming. Hang in there."*

*The syncopated whomp-whomp of helo blades reached his ears. He squinted into the sun, enough to see the dark hulking shape of a Chinook hovering several meters away. The feeling was leaving his leg, the cold numbness crawling up the rest of his body, and he knew it was too late.*

"Jonas," Shannyn said, reaching over and gripping his arm.

He turned his head, his eyes unfocused.

"Park! No!" He gave a mighty shout and leaped to his feet.

He paused and then without saying a single word, he ran up the embankment toward the truck.

Shannyn pulled back as if burned, shocked by his outburst and frightened, not for herself but for him. She knew without a doubt that he hadn't seen *her* when he'd looked into her eyes. She wanted to race after him, but she had Emma to worry about. "Honey, you pack up the food and I'll get the blanket, okay?" She ignored the stares of people around them and hastily folded the green blanket, gathering it and Jonas's jacket in her arms.

"What's wrong with Daddy?"

Shannyn gripped Emma's hand tightly. This was what she'd wanted to avoid. Putting Emma through any sort of stress. Shannyn should have known at their first meeting, when Emma had hit his leg. She should have known when he had those moments when time seemed to stop completely. Now Emma's face mirrored her own—concerned and frightened. Shannyn was torn between concern for Emma and worry for Jonas.

She paused a moment, squatted before Emma because she didn't know what frame of mind he'd be in when they got to the truck.

"I don't know for sure, Emma. But I think your daddy has some very bad memories. And I think that helicopter today reminded him of something bad, and he got scared."

"Daddies don't get scared."

Shannyn pulled her into a quick hug.

"Yes, honey, they sometimes do." She pulled away and held Emma by the arms, fighting to keep her own hands from trembling. "Mommies *and* daddies. Now, when we get back to the truck, Daddy might still be upset. So you're going to do exactly what I tell you, okay?"

"Yes, Mama," Emma replied meekly.

When Shannyn got there, Jonas was hanging on to the tailgate with one hand, his other hand braced on his thigh and his head hanging.

She approached carefully. "Jonas?"

When he looked up at her, all the color was drained from his face. Somehow he looked smaller. But he was reachable, she realized. She let out the breath she'd been holding.

"Emma, Daddy's fine. I'm going to talk to him, so you sit up in the truck, okay?"

She got Emma settled with the remainder of the lemonade.

"What happened?"

Jonas took long, restorative breaths, but they didn't help. Fear and shame overwhelmed him. Each day he went to work he told himself he was getting better. Even today, after the first flash, he'd convinced himself it was all fine. But it was a lie.

He'd told himself the debriefing he'd had with the shrink in Germany had been enough. Another lie. Never before had he had two episodes in the same day. Not even dealing with live fire exercises on base. It was something else and he couldn't put his finger on what was different now. It had been almost a year. Things were supposed to get better, not worse.

It had been easier when he hadn't felt anything. But lately…seeing Shannyn, remembering how he'd loved her, and now becoming involved with his daughter…he was feeling again. And feeling *something* meant feeling *everything*. Not just the here and now, and not just trying to fight his attraction to Shannyn. But everything he'd denied himself for nearly a year. Guilt, grief, resentment. Love.

Now she was waiting for him to explain, and he had no idea what to tell her.

"I need a minute." He took more breaths, willing his heart rate to calm completely as he searched for words.

"All right."

She couldn't understand. Didn't know what it was like out there. No one did unless they'd been through it. And who could he talk to? The only one who understood him was Parker. And

Parker was gone. Jonas closed his eyes, flooded with guilt and without the will to fight it.

She waited patiently for him, leaning against the door of the truck, and slowly he felt control slipping back, giving him enough strength to move out of the moment. He couldn't believe she was still standing there and not running. He remembered the feeling of thinking he was going to bleed to death and how his last thought had been that maybe he'd made a mistake leaving her. It was selfish. It had been selfish then and it was selfish now, but as the paralyzing fear drained away, all he was left with was need. For her.

When he looked into her face, it was with apology in every fiber.

"I am so sorry. What you must think…"

"We can worry about what I think later." She dismissed his apology with a hand. "We need to worry about you right now."

It was a fresh wound. He didn't want to be anyone's worry. It was his job to worry about others. To protect them. It was something he used to do very well, but lately he had done nothing but fail at it.

"I'm fine."

Her laugh was sharp with disbelief. "You can't possibly expect me to believe that. Oh, Jonas, you are so far from all right. You've slipped away before, but it's more than that, isn't it. More than you've let on."

He bristled. What did she know about it, anyway? She hadn't lived through it. She hadn't seen her best friend die. And he wouldn't wish that pain on anyone. As much as he wished he could lay his burden down, he knew that it wasn't fair for Shannyn and Emma to pay the price for his problems. He'd done a horrible job so far. The best thing he could do for them was protect them from the ugliness.

"It's for me to deal with."

Her lips formed a firm line and she waited five long seconds before speaking again.

"Not if you expect to have any sort of relationship with your daughter."

He was in no shape for her to be giving ultimatums. Sudden anger piled on top of the confusion left in the wake of his vivid flashback. It overrode the longing for her and the self-loathing he felt at his weakness, propelling him into action. He let go of the tailgate and squared his shoulders. "Don't threaten me, Shannyn."

She glanced into the truck and back at him. "Let me make it easy for you, Jonas. If you want to see Emma, you're going to have to let me help you. Even if it kills you."

Shannyn watched his fingers on the wheel, gripping as if his life depended on it. His jaw was set firmly; he gritted his teeth. He was furious with her. It came off him in angry waves.

She didn't care. Emma sat between them, her animated chatter of earlier silenced. She might only be five but Shannyn knew Emma got that something was wrong. It wasn't fair of them to put her in the middle of all their problems. From the first moment he'd shown up, Shannyn had a feeling that there would be nothing but trouble. But she hadn't anticipated it being this bad.

This wasn't just about them and their past relationship, although that was far from resolved. It was about Jonas and his health. And he could deny it all he wanted, but he needed help. She couldn't just wash her hands of him and send him away. There was Emma to consider. Despite knowing it would be simpler if she pushed him away, her heart couldn't let her do it. Not when he needed someone.

She sighed, licked her lips nervously. Who was she fooling? She wanted to help him, needed to. She cared what happened to him. She'd never really stopped caring for him. Today she'd had a glimpse of how good it could have been for all of them. And it had surprised her how natural it had felt, even after all these years. It was no longer a question of whether she'd done the right thing by keeping Emma a secret. They were a family of sorts now. Families stood by each other. Even when it hurt.

Just before they reached the house, she motioned to a small brick bungalow. "Pull in here," she said.

She took Emma with her and rang the bell.

When her neighbour, Patty, answered, Shannyn didn't beat around the bush. "Could Emma stay and play for a bit?"

Patty knit her brows. "You okay?"

"Yeah, but something came up. If it's too much of a bother…"

Patty looked down at Emma and back at Shannyn with a smile. "We're just having a Canada Day barbecue. Lisa's in the back playing by herself, so the company would be welcome."

"Thanks, Patty. I hope it won't be for long."

She knelt before Emma. "I'll be back to get you later, honey."

"Are you going to make Daddy feel better?"

Shannyn's smile wobbled at the concern on Emma's face. Her baby shouldn't have to worry about things like this. "I'm going to try. We need to talk about some things, that's all."

She stood and ruffled Emma's hair. "Thanks again," she said to Patty. She lifted a hand in farewell and jogged back to the truck where Jonas waited. Climbing into the cab, she knew he'd built a wall around himself. She could sense his isolation, see it in the cold, stony expression molding his features, the stiff way his hands gripped the steering wheel. Breaking through that wall wasn't going to be easy.

She unlocked the front door and led them into the quiet house.

"Shannyn, I'm sorry. I frightened Emma and upset you and ruined our day." The apology was perfunctory, devoid this time of true remorse. He was still behind that wall, giving her what he thought she needed to hear.

She turned at the kitchen counter. If she wanted answers, real ones, she was going to have to come at it strong, push her way through. "Yes, you did. And I want to know why."

He looked past her, through the window at the empty backyard. "It's complicated."

"I think I got that."

He turned his head a little and met her gaze. She knew he didn't want to talk about it. She also knew he had to let it out if they were going to move forward and establish some sort of status quo.

"Shannyn, you don't know what you're asking."

"I'm willing to take that chance."

"Maybe I'm not. Maybe I'm not willing to put you and Emma through this." He spun away, running his hand over the stubble on his jaw. But the veneer was starting to crack.

Shannyn looked at him. Why did he mean so much to her? It went so much deeper than the fact that he was Emma's father. She stared at his broad shoulders, the way his combat trousers sat on his hips. It was more than attraction to his physical perfection. She remembered the sight of the jagged scar running down his thigh, now marring that perfection. It wasn't sympathy, either.

The truth of the matter was, six years ago he'd been the first man she'd ever loved. She hadn't loved one since. And she knew she hadn't imagined their connection, no matter how he'd gone off and left her. There was something elemental between them, something tethering them together, and as much as she'd denied it to herself over the years, being with him again changed everything. It was his energy, the glimpses she got of it now and then. It was his sense of honor and his strength. It hurt her to see that strength tested; to see the battle he was waging with himself.

Their connection was as strong as ever. Perhaps even stronger. Too bad she'd already learned that the happily-ever-after she'd dreamed of as a child didn't really exist.

"Jonas, please look at me."

When he turned back around, her heart wept for the broken man before her. Whatever had happened, it was more than his leg being wounded. Something that would explain why he didn't consider himself a hero. Or why he kept distancing himself from her. Why he kept disappearing into himself.

"It's about time you trusted someone with it. And you know you can trust me."

"You'll look at me differently." His throat bobbed as he swallowed.

"Don't you know me better than that by now? I know you." She went forward, touched the hairline just above his ear with a tender hand. "I know you better than anyone. We might not like it, but it's true. Please let me in."

"Let's go outside. I need…I need space. And air."

She opened the patio doors and they went out, taking chairs on the tiny deck overlooking the yard.

"I don't know where to start." He leaned forward in the chair, resting his elbows on his knees, hands clasped.

Shannyn reached over and took his hand in hers. Somehow the simple contact linked them, more than just a handclasp. It was trust. Acceptance. A bond that went far deeper than attraction.

"Why don't you start with what it was like serving in Special Forces? We'll take it from there."

Jonas looked down at their joined hands. His was wide and scarred, hers slender, dainty. They were so different. Shannyn was being more than understanding. How much of that would change when he told her the truth? Would she look at him with shock, or derision? Yet, after today and his outburst at the air show, he knew he had to do something. It had been too long and the past was still stuck in the present. He had to move forward, somehow.

He pulled his hand away and started to get up. "Maybe it would be better if I talked to someone on base," he said, prevaricating. It was a weak argument and he knew it. But somehow he had to spare her the details. He didn't care what she said. When she knew what he'd done, she'd be disappointed at best. Disgusted, more likely.

"You don't need to protect me, Jonas. I grew a hard shell the day I realized I was pregnant and alone."

He sat back down. She didn't understand, not at all. Perhaps she would always hate him for leaving her behind. And he couldn't tell her the real reason why he'd left as he had. Maybe she was right. Maybe he did need to tell her what had happened. Once she knew what kind of man he really was, he wouldn't have to worry about protecting her in the future. Or worry about her getting ideas about them that wouldn't work. She'd send him packing and they could just move on to working out a visitation schedule.

She was strong. He got that. She had pulled herself up and had done a fine job of making a life for herself and Emma. But her lifestyle was far removed from the places he'd been or the things he'd seen. Even now, still dressed in her Canada Day colors, she was a picture of unspoiled beauty. He was anything but unspoiled. He was more convinced than ever that it wouldn't work between them.

Flirting had been fun. Kissing had been great. But today's episode reminded him very clearly why being with Shannyn was impossible, and why he'd insisted on being friends only. He'd allowed himself to forget. Telling her about Chris would create the distance he needed so he wouldn't have the power to hurt her again.

"You want to hear about what it was like?" His voice came out stronger than he thought possible. "I loved my job. Sure, it had its downside. In the Middle East it was hot and dusty, and there is a lot less glory to being a sniper than you'd imagine. You spend a lot of time waiting. And a lot of time isolated."

"But you had friends."

"Yeah."

He stopped, surprised at the lump that appeared in his throat. "You probably don't remember Chris Parker."

"The one from basic. Sandy-blond hair and devilish blue eyes."

He closed his eyes. She did remember him. And her description put a picture in his mind, one of Chris in full camouflage gear, his head tilted back and laughing. They'd constantly teased each other about nothing at all. It had been their one saving grace to get through the monotony of life there.

"Yes, that's him. He was my partner. Snipers work in pairs. Being with Chris…it was the closest I felt to being home. He was like a brother."

"Was?"

He couldn't look at her. "Yes, was. He was killed the day I was wounded."

He didn't know what he expected, but she simply said, "I'm sorry."

Shannyn angled her chair so she could see him and rested her arms on her knees, inviting him to continue. "Tell me."

A muscle in his jaw twitched, moving the tattoo on his cheek. The moment of fun, the touch of her fingers on his skin as she applied the sticker was far removed from their conversation now. The silence drew out for several beats.

"We were on assignment, nearly a year ago now. It was so hot it was like the sun had teeth. We were behind a knoll, over a mile from a village."

"Where?"

He chanced a look in her eyes before his gaze skittered away. "It doesn't matter where."

She translated it easily. "Covert."

"We waited over three hours for our mark to be in position. That day Chris was the spotter, I was the shooter."

Again he paused, taking his time, deciding what to tell. "When it was done, we hiked back to our rendezvous point and met up with the convoy that was to take us to the airfield."

He stopped, and at his silence she prodded gently, "What happened?"

He stared at a point somewhere past the back fence of the yard. "It had taken longer than we expected. There were… children involved. Children, Shan."

His haunted eyes probed hers, asking her to understand. "There were children there, holding guns. What kind of person gives a child a gun and gives them the burden of killing another human being?"

"I don't know."

He shook his head, as if he still couldn't believe it. "So we waited until the perfect time. But our delay meant the convoy was late getting out. I convinced them to take a shortcut, a different route. Chris and I were in the first vehicle, joking and laughing when we hit a landmine."

The picture threatened to take over again but he focused on her eyes, determined to go on with the story. "You have to understand…an Iltis is a light vehicle. It isn't built to withstand that sort of blast. We were thrown clear. The driver and the private beside him were wounded. My thigh was shattered, but Chris…Chris was dead."

When she looked at him, his eyes were filled with unshed tears. What she saw inside the shimmering depths cut her deeply. It wasn't just the loss of his best friend. The wound went so much deeper than simple grief. There was blame, regret, all pointed directly at himself.

"Seconds before, we'd been joking about his fiancée finding someone else. And because I insisted on a shortcut, he's gone. If I hadn't suggested that route, we never would have hit that mine and we'd both still be out there. My arrogance and impatience cost him his life."

Shannyn took her time answering, because she knew she had to get the words right. Oh, it was all so clear to her now. She could tell he was wearing guilt like a heavy shroud, carrying its weight every day. Feeling like he'd failed not only his friend but himself.

Quiet settled over the deck and birds sang. Shannyn wondered if birds still chirped in the places he'd been. How difficult it must be for him to come back to a place with such simple pleasures, to people who understood nothing of what he'd faced. She was one of those people. The least she could do was try.

Again she reached over and took his hand in hers.

"*You* didn't kill him, Jonas. It wasn't your fault."

"But it was. It was my decision. I wanted us to get a move on, get to the airfield and get out."

"And would there have been any guarantees that nothing would have happened if you'd gone the other way? Done things differently? Who's to say there wouldn't have been someone waiting to ambush you? The news is full of stories like that."

He shook his head stubbornly. "That's not the point. The point is, it was my decision, I made it, and now he's dead."

"You make it sound like you pulled the trigger."

"In a way I did."

She grabbed his other hand in hers and squeezed. "You look at me."

When he did, resistance masked his face. Oh, he was going to be a stubborn nut to crack. But now that she had an idea of what he was dealing with, she could at least help him move forward.

"You've been carrying this around ever since, haven't you."

When he didn't reply, she persisted. "This is eating you up inside, Jonas. I've been so focused on you and Emma that I didn't notice enough. I saw you were troubled but passed it off. But after today…I know it's not something you can ignore anymore. I think it's time you did something about it."

He sat up straighter, pulled his hands away, his brow wrinkling a bit in the middle. "What are you talking about, Shannyn?"

"What I'm talking about is getting you some professional help."

# CHAPTER ELEVEN

"A SHRINK? Don't be absurd."

Jonas got up from his chair and stalked to the door, sliding it open and escaping away from her, into the kitchen. She wished he wouldn't run away. Why couldn't he see that she was only trying to help him?

He had to know she was right. Shannyn got up and followed him.

"Jonas, you can't deal with this alone, and I'm pretty sure I can't help you the way you need. I had no idea it was this big. I knew you were different somehow. I could feel it. But you obviously can't go on this way."

"I can manage." He folded his arms in front of his chest.

"Jonas, for God's sake, put your pride away. I know you, remember? You're blaming yourself and it's tearing you apart. What would it hurt to talk to someone who deals with this sort of thing?" She went to a drawer and pulled out a phone book. She longed to reach out and touch him, but held back, knowing she had to stay focused on the issue at hand.

"Look, we can go through the yellow pages. Or maybe there's someone on base you can talk to. This has to be pretty common after a tough tour of duty, don't you think?"

She handed him the book, but to her frustration, he held it in his hands without looking at it. She reached out and grabbed his wrist, the contact sending a current to her toes.

Tears stung her eyes as she felt more torn than before. Wanting to be free of his hold on her and needing to help him was all mixed up with what was best for Emma. He could be so stubborn. "Please, Jonas," she whispered, squeezing his hand. "You need to get help. Your leg is nearly healed. But you're still hurting inside."

"I can't go there, I'm sorry." He pulled away and put the book down on the counter. But she noticed his hands were shaking.

"You're scared." She shook her head at him. "Don't worry, I'm not going to take out a billboard or put an announcement in the paper. I'm just saying you should talk to someone who knows how to help you the way I can't."

"And let it get around the base?"

Obstinate. For a moment she wondered how many soldiers came back to the same thing and were too proud or ashamed to get the help they needed. Tough guys that thought they could handle it alone. But she couldn't be concerned about others. She needed to help this man. The father of her child. The man she'd once loved.

"Then go off base. Find an independent doctor."

He started pacing, his hands braced on his hips. His gait was stiff, like he'd suddenly tensed everything in his body. Now that she knew about Chris Parker everything fit. And that was only one incident over the course of several years. How many other demons haunted him? It would be naive to think that he hadn't had other experiences that affected him deeply. Perhaps not as much as that of the death of his friend, but cumulatively…no wonder he was a mess. She wanted to take the pain away for him, but knew she was helpless to do so. Her only hope was to make him see that he needed it for himself.

He stopped pacing and looked at her. Every one of his features held some measure of pain.

"Why are you doing this? To keep me away from Emma? Are you angry about the other day? Why are you punishing me?" His arm swept wide, anger his new armor.

"Of course I'm not punishing you. You're doing a fine job of punishing yourself."

"I don't believe you. You wanted to keep Emma from me all along. And when you couldn't anymore, you decided to…"

His gaze changed suddenly, calculating, assessing her. "That's it, isn't it. You're angry about what I said Thursday. About being just friends."

The abrupt change in him threw her off balance. What did he mean? This was about him and the disturbing flashbacks. It had nothing to do with her.

"What are you talking about?"

"You came on to me during my session. And when that didn't work, you kept it up during coffee. Only it didn't turn out the way you wanted."

Her mouth dropped open. "That's ridiculous. I'd never do something so manipulative."

"You don't think keeping Emma from me was manipulative? Why in the world would I trust you?"

Shannyn's lip quivered. Didn't he understand how important this was? She could barely get the words out. "How did this suddenly become about me?"

"You're the one who had a secret. If I hadn't shown up, I still wouldn't know about Emma. So don't pretend my problems matter to you." He braced his hands on his hips, looking satisfied with himself.

"Of course you matter to me!"

"Because of Emma."

"Not only because of Emma!"

"Now we're getting somewhere. Why don't you just admit what you want, Shannyn."

"I don't understand."

"I'm talking about this."

He took three giant strides, swept her up and pressed his lips to hers.

And, oh, he felt good. Tasted good. Like tart lemon and sweet sugar blended with a flavor that was simply Jonas. Her arms were pinned against her sides as he crushed her close, kissing her and making every nerve ending in her body thrum with hope.

Hope.

Hope would be the worst mistake she could make.

"Stop." She pulled her way out of his arms, walking backward until she was blocked by the stove. "Stop this. This doesn't change anything."

His lips curved craftily. "Oh, I think it does. I know how you felt just now." His voice was silky, seductive. "What you were feeling. You wanted me."

A shiver teased over her body. But she knew now that it was his way of diverting the topic. And she had to press on. It was too important.

"No, Jonas. Not like this. We have issues to work out. I know that. But today is not the time. Today is about something bigger."

The sexy smile disappeared as quickly as it had appeared.

"Jonas, no one can go through what you did without having some sort of lingering effect." She put the topic back on track. "You need to put it behind you. You do."

"I just want to forget about it. I didn't misread what happened just now. You can help me forget." His eyes communicated tacit suggestions on how that might be accomplished.

Shannyn wanted to cry. If he only knew how desperately she

wanted to make love with him. Knowing the reality of their situation had nothing to do with longings, and she had those aplenty. She remembered how it had been between them. Had imagined how it could be again, to her growing consternation.

If only healing were that simple. But damage had been done and she didn't see how it could be fixed. And to use it as a method of running away…she wasn't so naive. She knew it would only lead to more hurt. What she secretly wanted…the three of them together…that would never happen.

"You'll never forget, Jonas, and you know that. You need to find a way to make peace with it, not make it disappear." If only she could take her own advice.

She knew she'd gotten through to him when he exhaled and put a hand over his face.

She went to him. For right now the rest didn't matter. She laid her fingers on his shoulder and softly put her other hand over his and drew it down so his face was uncovered once more. "Please let me help you. Don't you know you're safe with me?"

The shoulder beneath her hand trembled and she struggled to hold back tears, longing for him to trust her this much. She let her fingers soothe their way down his arm, feeling the firm muscle beneath the warm skin.

"I care about what happens to you, Jonas. Not for Emma. Not for myself. For you." She halted, afraid of the next words but saying them, anyway. "Can't you see you're still in my heart?"

His breath caught. She felt him hold it in. She was so close to getting the rest of the way through. "If you can't do it yourself, then let me be the strong one. You've fought for so long. Please, let me fight for you this one time. All you have to do is hold on."

"I don't know how to do that," he admitted quietly.

"Just trust in me for once. Let go and start at the beginning and we'll do it together, I promise."

His arms snaked around her, pulling her close, cinching her tightly against him. She wrapped her arms around his ribs and held on, feeling their strength coming together. Accepting that together they were so much stronger than they were individually.

The sun had moved and was shining through the side window of the kitchen when Jonas stepped back and out of her arms.

"I'm sorry," he murmured, not looking at her.

"No," she answered strongly. "No more sorry. You needed to get it out."

"I wanted to spare you the ugly parts. I didn't want you to know."

Shannyn rested her hand on his cheek and peered into his face. "But I wanted to share them with you. I'm glad you told me, Jonas. It explains so much. It's going to get better now, you'll see."

He put his hand over hers, and she smiled up at him. "I can't promise to understand all of it. I wasn't there. But I'll do my best. It's going to get better," she repeated. "That I *can* promise."

He sighed, pursing his lips and looking away. "It already it is better. I'm the one who's alive. He isn't."

"And punishing yourself won't bring him back." She put her right hand on his other cheek, forcing him to look into her eyes. "I still think you need to talk to a professional. Someone who knows how to deal in this particular area of trauma."

"I don't need a shrink to tell me what I need, Shan. Spouting a bunch of touchy-feely gobbledygook."

"Do you want to live like this for the rest of your life, then?"

He pulled away from her hands. "You know what? I can't think of that now. It's been such a roller-coaster day. Right now I'm just tired."

Shannyn suppressed a sigh. One conversation was not going to fix this and make everything all right for him. It would take time. He needed time. She knew that sharing as much as he had must have been exhausting. She merely nodded.

"Of course you are."

"I should talk to Emma, though. I don't want her last memory of today being that of me flipping out." He sighed. "You and me…we've talked about it. You understand. But Emma doesn't."

Shannyn was glad. Not only for Emma—it was good that he was considering their daughter's feelings—but for herself. It would be a way to keep him close a little longer today. To perhaps convince him to get the help he needed.

"Why don't you lie down in the living room and rest? I'll go get Emma from Patty's in a bit, and we'll have a quiet dinner together. The three of us." She put her hands in the pockets of her shorts and tried to sound normal.

"That sounds good. More than good." He attempted a small smile and nearly succeeded.

"It's the least I can do. And I agree. I think it's important for Emma to see you again, to see that you're okay." She hesitated. "Jonas…you promise you won't leave?" She didn't quite trust him. She could very well go to pick up Emma and come home to an empty house.

"Are you kidding? If I tried to pull that, you'd be at my door in ten minutes."

Shannyn laughed. "Yes, I would. Besides, I think we could both use a regular evening after the events of the day."

"You're probably right. I'll lie down for a bit and then we'll have dinner and I'll make it up to Emma for ruining her afternoon."

When Shannyn came back with Emma, Jonas was asleep on the couch, his body so long that his feet hung over the curved arm at the end. One arm was bent and under his head, the opposite hand resting on the cushions in front of his abdomen.

When he slept, his troubles all seemed to vanish from his face. Like when they'd met Corporal Benner, he seemed younger. Freer.

"Daddy's sleeping," she whispered to Emma, holding her hand. For some reason, the word *Daddy* no longer seemed foreign on her tongue. It belonged. Like Jonas did.

She knelt down before Emma and squeezed her hand. "Let's make him a special supper, okay? And we'll all eat together and have ice cream sandwiches for dessert."

Emma nodded enthusiastically. "Can we make hot dogs?"

Shannyn laughed. To a five-year-old, hot dogs *did* constitute a special meal. "Sure, pumpkin. Hot dogs it is. And maybe a potato salad and your favorite veggies and dip."

At Emma's broad smile Shannyn put on her mock stern face. "But this is a team effort, young lady. You've got to pull your weight."

"Yes, ma'am," Emma replied. She giggled. "That's what Daddy says."

Shannyn pulled Emma in for a hug. Jonas, with all his problems, was already becoming a part of the family, an influence on Emma's life. And this was only the beginning. She had no idea where things were going to lead with him. No matter how he denied it, his kisses didn't lie. The connection she felt didn't lie. The fact that he trusted her with the truth, and that she was beginning to trust him more every day, brought them closer together. It complicated *everything*.

A sigh escaped as she released Emma and turned to the refrigerator. She didn't want to care, didn't want to need him. It would be so much simpler if she didn't. If only they could agree to parent Emma separately. If only she could turn her residual feelings off.

She put potatoes on to boil for salad and as she cut vegetables, Emma arranged them on a pretty plate. Together they mixed the potatoes and dressing and she let Emma sprinkle the paprika on the top. She lit the barbecue and got out a pack of hot dogs, leaving Emma to carry out the condiments and plastic dishes.

Emma came back inside for plates and cutlery and slid the patio door shut with far too much force than necessary. It banged loudly against the frame, the harsh slam echoing through the house.

Shannyn jumped, then jumped again as a horrific shout and crash came from the living room. Without thinking, she rushed around the corner, Emma on her heels, and the sight that greeted her froze her to the spot.

Jonas stood in the middle of the floor, his chest pumping heavily and the coffee table overturned. Picture frames and her favorite vase lay scattered on the floor.

"Jonas! My God, what happened?"

His head turned, nothing else. Shannyn took a step backward at the sight of his cold eyes. Now she knew what he'd meant when he'd said he wanted to spare her the details. There was a dark side he hadn't wanted her to see. The Jonas before her now wasn't the same man she'd held in her arms earlier. At Emma's whimper, she automatically put her arm out, pulling Emma close to her side, comforting her.

Jonas stared at them blankly. The dream was still so real. Vignettes and faces that made little sense, and then cut to the hospital in Germany. He'd been shouting to the doctor about Chris's body and then suddenly he'd been screaming that it was Shannyn's body and he'd broken his promise…

Now, slowly, slowly her face registered. As the fog cleared, he realized he was standing in Shannyn's living room. She was staring at him with horror etched on every feature. Eyes wide, mouth open, face pale.

Behind her right hip stood Emma, wearing the same expression but with an added emotion he recognized. He'd seen it before. More than he cared to recall.

She was afraid. Not just frightened but afraid of *him*.

He looked away, only to register the chaos created by his

outburst. The silk flowers in the vase were scattered in a tangle of red, orange and green. The coffee table was on its side. A picture frame lay facedown, but bits of broken glass peeked from beneath the wooden frame. He didn't remember jumping up. Didn't remember knocking the table over.

He turned back to Shannyn and Emma. This was so wrong. They both deserved so much better. But especially Emma. She didn't understand any of this. "I'm sorry," he tried, but the words came out choked. He cleared his throat. "Emma…"

But Emma spun around and ran from the room. Her footsteps pounded on the stairs, and moments later her bedroom door slammed.

Shannyn glanced at the stairs and then back at Jonas, undecided.

"You were right, Shan. About everything." His voice was quiet and broken in the silent aftermath of his outburst. "Go to Emma while I clean up this mess. While I get my head on straight. I need to talk to both of you."

Shannyn quietly did what he asked. She turned and walked away from him, up the stairs to Emma. It was the right thing for her to do. Emma needed her mother now more than anything.

He squatted and picked up the picture, careful of the broken glass. It was a five by seven of Shannyn and Emma together. Shannyn's arms were looped around Emma's neck, both of them smiling. A set of blue eyes and a set of green, both with a dusting of freckles on their noses.

Carefully he righted the table and then placed the pieces of glass on it gently. He'd broken their family as surely as he'd broken the picture, just by being here.

This was why Shannyn hadn't told him about Emma. He understood that now. And he knew that somehow he had to make it right. It was too late for him to walk away. Emma wouldn't understand him leaving now.

Hell, he wouldn't understand, if it came to that.

He'd made a promise to be a father, and he wasn't going to break it. And Shannyn… Somehow he had to find a way to fix it for all of them. No more running away.

He picked up the vase, held it gingerly in his hands before placing it precisely in the middle of the table. The nightmares weren't going away any more than the flashes of memory were. Today had been the worst day since it had happened.

In this one he'd dreamed it was Shannyn at the end and he'd overturned a doctor's trolley trying to find her. It didn't take a rocket scientist to realize that she was there because he'd started caring about her again. He could bluster and protest all he wanted, the truth was he cared about her. In his heart he knew he wasn't coping very well. With losing Chris or with losing Shannyn.

Shannyn's footsteps came back down the stairs and he straightened, his hand full of silk flowers. He put them on the table too when she came back in the room.

She'd put everything on the line for him today, even though he'd been a complete jerk, using whatever feelings she had for him against her. No matter where they ended up, at the very minimum she would always be a part of his life because of Emma. And he'd hurt her enough over the years. He knew that. He was done with hurting her. It was time for him to attempt to make things right.

"You were right." He began the conversation by taking responsibility for all of it. "I can't do this by myself. I need help and I'm going to get it. I can't do this to you and Emma."

Shannyn crossed the floor in quick steps, wrapping her arms around his neck and pressing her cheek to his chest. Slowly he put his arms around her, unsure of what to do. She was crying. He could tell by the irregular jolt of her chest against his, the hint of wetness that clung to his shirt. It wasn't what he'd expected.

She should be shouting at him, kicking him out after what he'd done! Instead she was giving him acceptance and comfort.

"Why aren't you afraid?" he whispered into her ear, overcome. "God, Shan, you should be afraid."

Her head shook against him. "No. I'm not afraid *of* you, Jonas. I'm afraid *for* you. If you mean it about getting help, I'm relieved. It kills me to see you in so much pain."

"But I scared you both so much."

"We'll be fine. And you will, too."

She was so strong, so willing to give of herself. She always had been. In some strange way, it made him proud. At that moment he couldn't think of a woman he'd rather have as a mother to his daughter.

Shannyn stepped back, sniffing and swiping a finger beneath her lashes.

"Don't you see, Jonas? This is a beginning. A new one for you. Why would I be upset about that?"

# CHAPTER TWELVE

W HEN the hot dogs were almost ready, Shannyn called Emma down for supper.

Jonas was waiting for Emma outside, nervously bouncing his knee as he sat at the picnic table. He'd spoken to Shannyn, but she was glad he felt he owed Emma an explanation, too. His respect for her feelings, and for Emma's, told her he meant what he said about getting help.

Shannyn was relieved to find Emma subdued but not afraid when she came downstairs. "Your dad wants to talk to you, honey. Do you think you can do that?"

Emma nodded, looking suddenly far older than her five years.

Shannyn watched the scene outside unfold with a lump in her throat. Dinner was ready, but Emma and Jonas needed this time together. Hot dogs and potato salad could wait.

Jonas talked to Emma, his face sober and honest. For a minute they remained a few feet apart. Then Emma held out her bear— the one she called Mr. Huggins—and he took it into his hands.

Emma's arms went around her father and Shannyn pressed a hand to her mouth. Children were so forgiving. Seeing Jonas come apart at the seams had frightened her to death. But her fear had instantly become secondary once she realized he'd been trapped in his own personal hell.

And Emma had been crying when she'd gone upstairs to check on her. Explaining hadn't been easy, but Shannyn had tried to keep it simple. Daddy had nightmares sometimes, and he'd had one today. He wasn't angry at her, or at Shannyn. It wasn't Emma's fault.

She ran her fingertips over her lips, unable to forget the passion in his kiss.

When Jonas and Emma pulled apart, Shannyn saw Jonas turn his head to wipe his eyes privately before turning a smile on Emma. He'd made everything right. She was surprised to find tears in her own eyes, and wiped her lashes. Clearing her throat, she picked up the tray holding their food and went to the patio door. When she knocked on the window, Emma bounced up to open it. Even though Jonas was awake, Shannyn noticed how gently Emma closed the door behind her.

"Supper's ready, guys," she called out, and had to work to paste on a smile. What a topsy-turvy day it had turned out to be.

Jonas got up to help her, taking the tray from her hands, his warm fingers brushing over hers. "Is there more?"

"Yes, there are a few more things on the counter."

He placed the tray on the picnic table and then followed her inside. She grabbed the pitcher of lemonade but before she could go back out, he put his hand on her arm.

"Thank you," he said, his voice low. It sent shivers up her spine. "Whatever you said to Emma upstairs, it worked. She's strong, Shan. She gets that from you."

Shannyn closed her eyes. Every time he touched her now it seemed all her senses kicked in. Each touch, each caress seemed loaded with deeper meaning. He'd verbally thrown a lot of things at her this afternoon, but she was smart enough to know they had only been a smokescreen. Now every moment, every revelation into his character, drew her closer. Intertwined their lives. It elated her almost as much as it frightened her.

"Don't credit me. I saw you through the window. You clearly said the right thing. She *never* shares Mr. Huggins."

He let her arm go, and she turned to open the door.

"Shan?"

When she faced him again, he was holding glasses in his hands. For a second she got an intuitive feeling, as if he were going to say something she wouldn't like. He looked almost apologetic.

"I know what I've got to do."

He slid past her out into the yard before she could ask him what he meant.

They sat at the table, reminiscent of a regular family ritual. Plates were filled, chatter ensued. Shannyn stole glances at Jonas. He acted as if he was fine; he laughed and smiled and ate like all was normal. But Shannyn couldn't shake the feeling that somehow something was wrong. What did he feel he had to do? And why was he waiting to tell her?

The evening was waning, settling into mellow sunset when they unwrapped ice cream sandwiches. Shannyn handed around napkins as chins sported dribbles of vanilla and chocolate. Jonas sighed.

"What is it?"

Jonas looked into her eyes. She wondered again if she saw remorse in his hazel depths or if she only imagined it. He held her gaze for a long time, reached out and squeezed her free hand, then pulled away and cleared his throat.

"I want you both to know that I might not be around as much for a while."

Shannyn put down what was left of her sandwich, blindly wiping her fingers on a paper napkin. What was left of her appetite had diminished completely. This was it, then. She'd overstepped after all, and he was backing away. After all that had happened, he was clearing out. Just like last time.

"Why, Daddy?" Emma voiced the question for both of them.

Jonas smiled at Emma, a wistful turn of his lips. "You know my dream today? I get them a lot. And your mom and I think it would be good if I got some help."

"Help from who?" Emma took a bite of her sandwich, her eyebrows raised in innocent curiosity.

"Help from a doctor, sweetheart."

Shannyn's heart gave a solid thump. He had meant it, then. He was going to get help. She was glad. Glad for him, but selfishly couldn't help but think that if she were interpreting right, he was doing it alone. She'd begged him to do it, but now couldn't help but feel left behind.

They'd come so far, and they'd done it together. Sometimes fighting, sometimes crying, but he'd shared it with her. She didn't quite understand why he was withdrawing from them now. Perhaps her heart would be safer, but not Emma's. She balled up the napkin, fussing with it, wanting to ask the questions but knowing they needed to be voiced in private, not in front of Emma.

"Do you have to go away for that? Will he give you a needle?"

Jonas laughed. "No, and I hope not."

"Then why are not going to be here?" Her lips formed a tiny pout. "I start soccer this week. I wanted you to come."

*Thank you, Emma,* Shannyn thought. She was wondering the same thing. Why did getting help preclude him being with them? She knew that if *she* were to ask, he'd find a way to avoid answering. It was harder for him to put off Emma's innocent questions.

Jonas got up from his side of the table and moved over to sit beside Emma. He took her sticky hand in his. "I'm not going to be gone completely. I just won't be here regularly. I need some time to figure things out, that's all. So I can get better, and be a better daddy to you." He halted, then lifted his hand and grazed her cheek with a finger. "I don't want what happened today to happen again. It hurt me to see you scared." His eyes darted up to Shannyn's. "To see you both scared."

Shannyn saw the logic in what he was saying even as her heart rebelled against it. It was the responsible thing to do, she supposed. She wanted him well, she truly did. But she didn't understand his need to avoid them while he was doing it. They could help him, she was sure of it. He'd already said that Emma helped him. What she'd feared would come true. He would withdraw and she'd be left to answer Emma's questions about why Daddy wasn't around.

Emma wasn't the only one who would miss him. Shannyn admitted to herself what she wouldn't to another soul. She would miss Jonas; the sound of his voice, the way he bounced his knee without realizing he was doing it. The way he ran his hand over the stubble of his military cut or rubbed his bad leg when he got upset.

"I'm sure your daddy will come for visits, honey." Her eyes fell on Jonas, telegraphing a look that said, *You'd better.*

She wished she could read his thoughts. When his gaze locked with hers, they seemed to acknowledge what she'd said. And when he spoke, he spoke to her, even though the words were meant for Emma.

"I'm not leaving you. That I promise."

Her heart lifted. He meant it. She was suddenly sure of it.

There was still so much to say. She longed to know what he was going to do, when she would see him again.

"Let's take this stuff inside and run you a bath, Emma. You're sticky from one end to the other."

"I'll get it," Jonas offered. He stood and began piling dishes on the tray. "You get Emma in the tub." He smiled at Emma. "Then I'll read you a story before bed."

When Shannyn came back downstairs, he was putting the supper mess away. It felt right, having him there in her kitchen.

She smiled a little, remembering how she'd first considered him an intruder into their lives. But now…now she was beginning to believe she could trust him to keep his word. He was getting the help he needed. He was taking a genuine interest in Emma. She couldn't ask for more than that.

"Thanks for tidying up."

He turned from the sink. "You're welcome. It's the least I could do after the day I put you through."

"What are you going to do now, Jonas?" She leaned against the breakfast nook.

"I don't know."

That made her frown. "But you think withdrawing from us is a good idea?"

Jonas put down the dishcloth and rested his hips against the counter so that they were facing each other in the contained space. "How can you ask that, after today?"

"I think today has shown you that we're tougher than we look." She stood straighter, her back coming off the resting spot. Why couldn't he see that it wasn't she and Emma that needed to be protected here?

Jonas folded his arms. "Today taught me that it's not fair for me to expect you to deal with my problems. Today it was a nightmare. A broken picture, an overturned table. What if it had been different? What if you'd come in and had shaken me to wake me up?

"I don't trust myself, Shan. And I never want to see that look on Emma's face again. I realized I'm unpredictable. I don't know what will trigger a memory, a flash. Today is the worst day I've had. Twice at the air show I lost time. I'll admit it now. And then after all that, the nightmare. Until I know it's okay, I don't want to chance scaring her again." His face softened. "Scaring you."

"Going away is hurting us. Emma won't understand." She let

her gaze skitter away, as she admitted, "I…I don't understand. I thought I helped you. I thought…I thought we'd agreed that we'd be friends." The idea sounded so odd from her lips. They meant more to each other than friends, yet somehow even friendship seemed elusive between them. They'd built a tenuous truce, that was all.

"You did help me. But you were right about one thing. I need more than time and a friendly shoulder. I promise I'll make time for some contact. I'll pick Emma up and we'll go for an ice cream. I'll come to a soccer game. But not…not a scheduled, prolonged thing. Please try to understand. I need to do this. I need to get things clear, and you…you complicate things."

After what they'd been through together today, all she'd wanted was some quiet time for them to just *be*. To maybe sit quietly in the shade of the maple tree and unwind, to let the day settle and drift away on the evening breeze. To be held in his arms, secure. Safe. Instead he was talking about walking away. Putting *more* distance between them rather than drawing closer.

Shannyn felt the quiver in her stomach, a little sliver of fear. She'd already begun to rely on him, to get too involved. Even tonight she'd started to trust him again. Longing to be held in his arms. He'd never given the impression he truly wanted more. A few kisses and a whole lot of arguments did not translate into rebuilding a relationship.

The last time she'd trusted him he'd gone away for good. Perhaps he was right. Maybe a little distance would let everyone regain their balance. Moving slower wouldn't hurt. She was wrong about not needing protection. Maybe she did need it, but not from him. From herself. From letting herself feel more than was prudent. It was for the best.

Except that it already hurt. Each time she felt them get closer, the fear that he'd eventually leave her again was like a crack that spread under pressure.

Emma's footsteps came down the stairs. She was shiny-faced and in a blue-and-white nightdress, a brush in her hands.

"Mommy. I'm ready for you to brush my hair."

Shannyn looked back at Jonas. "Do what you have to do," she murmured, then moved to take the brush from Emma's hand.

Jonas picked up the paper cups and opened the truck door with a finger. One year. Exactly one year had passed since they'd driven over the landmine, and it was time to face a few things.

He shut the truck door with a jut of his hip, holding the hot coffee in shaking hands. His therapist had said this would be a good idea. The doc had also said he was making progress. Right now, with his stomach churning and his body trembling, he wasn't so sure of that. But he'd promised Shannyn he'd get help, and so here he was. Four hours from home in a small town in Nova Scotia.

He put one foot in front of the other until he reached the gate, swinging it open with a rusty creak.

It wasn't hard to find the headstone. It was slightly larger than the others, with a maple leaf adorning the top. For a minute he stood staring at it, at the words carved in gray stone.

He took one of the coffees and put it down beside the monument. "I brought you a double-double," he said quietly, referring to the familiar term for two cream and two sugars from Tim Hortons. Feeling awkward, he flipped back the plastic on his own cup to reveal the drinking spout and took a hesitant sip.

He'd been afraid that seeing Chris's name here, seeing the date, he'd be inundated with memories and painful flashes. But there was none of it. Only a deep sorrow that he'd lost his best friend.

"I'm sorry, Park," he whispered. He squatted down so he was

at eye level with the epitaph. "I'm sorry. And I miss you." He smiled a little. "That's all."

"Sgt. Kirkpatrick."

He rose and spun, coffee flying out of the small hole in the lid. "Nessa."

She smiled sadly. "You know who I am."

"Park carried your picture everywhere." She was even more beautiful in person, he realized. Creamy skin, dark hair flowing around her shoulders, brown eyes that seemed to really see him and held a note of sorrow he recognized.

"How are you holding up, Sgt.?"

Jonas looked back at the headstone. "I'm here. I'm fine."

She came forward, putting down a handful of mixed flowers. She caught sight of the cup and covered her mouth, suddenly laughing.

"Oh, how he loved his morning coffee with you. What a lovely tribute, Jonas."

It was odd, feeling so connected to someone he'd never met. "I've had some trouble getting over what happened," he admitted, surprised he was able to talk about it without feeling like he was strangling. "So I drove down to see him. To apologize. That sounds stupid," he finished.

Nessa put her hand on his arm. "Not at all. You never got to say goodbye. I can't imagine what you went through. If this is what you need to move on…"

"But you lost a fiancé. A future. I'm so sorry for that." Despite counseling, he still couldn't completely erase the feeling of responsibility that haunted him for denying this woman a husband.

She smiled at him then, a soft understanding. "It wasn't your fault. I know that. It was what happened and he's gone. He lived for the Army. I knew it and wanted him, not even despite it, but maybe even because of it. It was so much of who he was." Her soft eyes shone with the love she still felt. "I've accepted it, Jonas."

"But knowing what you know now, would you have done it? Would you have been with him knowing he would be killed?"

The question had been on his mind a lot lately. Being with Shannyn, and experiencing all the old feelings, had made him wonder about the woman Chris had left behind. Nessa was a living example of exactly what Jonas had tried to protect Shannyn from. He'd done what he thought he had to do, what was best. But now he was more involved in Shannyn's life than before. He had a daughter, and he was beginning to doubt everything he'd believed. Was starting to think he'd had it all wrong in the first place.

She hugged her arms around herself. "Yes, I would. Even with the pain...loving him was beautiful. I'm grateful for the time we had. I wouldn't trade a second of it. He made me a better person."

She faced the grave, a wistful smile curving her lips. "He was the most *alive* person I ever knew. Yes, it hurts. It still does and I think of him every day. But my life was better for having him in it. And I know he wouldn't want me to grieve forever. He'd want me to go on and have a fabulous life. To be happy. So I try to spend every day living up to that."

Jonas swallowed. It was simple and the most beautiful tribute he'd ever heard. It fit his memories of Chris perfectly.

Nessa reached down and took his hand, lifting it up between them. "Do you think he'd want anything less for you, Jonas? You, his best friend? Do you think he'd want you to spend your life blaming yourself? Denying yourself happiness because you feel guilty that you're here and he's not?"

Jonas choked on a laugh while tears filled his eyes. "He'd tell me to shut up and get on with it. And probably a few other choice words."

"Then why aren't you?"

He stared into her eyes. Why wasn't he? She was right. She

was absolutely right. What sort of tribute was *he* paying his friend? Chris would say he was alive but not living and he'd be right.

There were two girls back in Fredericton who deserved more than he'd been giving. He'd been foolish to try to engineer things in the first place. He'd played God with Shannyn's life thinking he was doing the right thing, but he knew now he'd been wrong. He had held on to the anger about Emma's paternity to avoid facing the fact that his feelings for her hadn't changed at all. Tried putting all the blame on her to keep her at arm's length. But the truth was, he wasn't really that mad about it anymore. They'd both spent so long being afraid that it was all they knew.

He had to see her. Had to tell her what he'd really done six years ago when he'd left for Edmonton, and tell her he was sorry. Knowing it, and for once *not* being afraid of it gave him a sense of freedom he hadn't known for many years.

He turned to Nessa, who was watching him with a broad smile. As everything became crystal clear, his lips curved up in response. "You are one hell of a woman. Chris always said so and now I know he was right. You have no idea what you've just done for me." He let out a giant breath. "Thank you. Thank you so much."

"Be happy, Jonas," she replied, leaning up and kissing his cheek. "Chris would want that for you."

Jonas turned back to the monument and lifted his hand in salute. His chest filled, his back straightened, his chin lifted.

When he passed Nessa, he put a hand on her shoulder, then broke into a jog as he headed out the gate and back to the woman he loved.

# CHAPTER THIRTEEN

AMIDST the happy shouts and whistles, he saw Shannyn. On the sidelines of the field, clapping her hands, engrossed in the game. The dying sun gleamed off her hair, warmed the skin of her arms to an amber glow. For a few moments Jonas watched, saw Emma running up the field in her yellow-and-white shirt, following the ball, joined by a handful of identically dressed children.

He'd made so many mistakes. So many decisions based on fear and not enough based on faith. And in the face of it all she'd somehow found the strength to help him when she thought he needed it.

What made him qualified to decide what was best for Shannyn? He'd loved her all along and had pushed her away out of fear. Not anymore. He'd been gone for too long. Six long years they'd wasted.

He was home. They were his. It was time he started taking the steps to claim them.

As if she could read his thoughts, she turned, her body suddenly backlit by the sunset, golden and gorgeous.

He had so much to tell her. About what he'd been doing over the past weeks. About what he'd done earlier today. About what he envisioned for the future.

Shannyn turned, her heart catching at the sight of Jonas

staring. He was all long legs and broad shoulders in faded jeans and a green T-shirt with a small crest on the chest. When he started walking toward her, his limp was indiscernible.

She stepped off the sidelines, retreating from the cheering crowd a little. His eyes locked with hers, his strides purposeful.

In that moment it became very clear. She loved Jonas. She always had, even when he'd come back and turned her life upside down with demands. Even when she'd seen him struggle with demons that frightened her. And especially now, watching him walk toward her. For her it would always be him.

He stopped in front of her, and it took everything she possessed not to launch herself into his arms. Blood rushed into her cheeks and she covered them with her hands, laughing softly. What was she thinking? There were at least twenty impressionable children around as well as parents and coaches. She'd never been much into public displays of affection. As much as she wanted to, she held back. This wasn't the place, even if it did feel like the right time.

"We didn't expect you tonight." Her words came out on a soft rush of breath. "Emma will be ecstatic."

"I hope it's okay that I came." Her eyes were drawn to his lips as they formed the words. "I have so much to tell you. So much to explain."

Shannyn lifted her chin and held his hands tightly as she looked deeply into his eyes. "I'm glad. I've been waiting…"

"I know. And I'm sorry I've made you wait so long."

"It's all right. I knew you were trying to get better."

"No." He shook his head. "I don't mean just now. This is so much bigger than me dealing with grief and stress. I mean from the beginning. I shouldn't have made you wait." The pressure of his fingers on hers tightened. "I…oh, hell. I need to tell you some things, things I should have said a long time ago."

He *had* done some serious soul searching, then. Shannyn kept her hands within his.

She thought back to the rare times over the past weeks that he'd carved out time to spend with them. He'd kept it simple then, too. An ice-cream cone, watching one of Emma's games. She'd known he was getting help, but he had distanced himself as he said he would.

But tonight…something had changed. Tonight he looked like a man set free. There was something more. Hope slammed into her. She wasn't imagining their connection. Could it be he felt the same way and he wanted to tell her? What was it that had happened that had caused this transformation?

"Each time I've seen you, you've seemed taller. Stronger. And I've wanted to ask you so many times…"

The shriek of a whistle cut through the air, ending the game and halting their conversation.

"Mama, Mama! Did you see me?" Emma came barreling off the field, ponytail bobbing, a streak of dirt gracing the sleeve of her shirt. Then she saw Jonas and squealed, "Daddy!"

Shannyn didn't have time to caution her to slow down. Emma raced straight at Jonas.

She needn't have worried. Jonas hefted her in the air, dirt and all, laughing. "Hey, angel! How was the game?"

"It was great. I almost scored."

"Good for you." He plopped a kiss on her nose, grinning broadly.

Shannyn's eyes widened. He was so open tonight, so giving. Without the wall he'd put around himself. Seeing him this way was like waking up. Like seeing the first crocuses blooming in the midst of the late-winter snow. Defiant beauty through cold ice. He'd always warmed to Emma, but this was more than that.

This was the Jonas she remembered. The man she'd fallen in love with. Having him back only made the feelings more intense.

"You ready to go home?"

Emma's face fell. "Aren't you coming?"

His eyes softened as he smiled tenderly at his daughter.

"Of course I'm coming. I'll tuck you in tonight and then I'm going to have a talk with your mom."

"Goody!"

Shannyn laughed even as her heart skipped. "We'd better get going, then. I promised Em a treat after the game. And then it's bedtime for you, silly girl."

Shannyn looked at Jonas, a secret thrill rushing through her as his eyes warmed on her. They would talk. She knew she should keep the topic away from their personal relationship. As happy as she was to see the old Jonas new again, so many things hadn't changed. They would need time to talk about what had just happened. About what was changing inside him. About what needed to happen in the future, for all of them. They had work to do, but for the first time, she knew that somehow they'd find a way.

Emma ran ahead to Shannyn's car, but Jonas stayed with Shannyn, his hand a warm anchor on her back. She wasn't sure she could trust herself to stay on topic if he kept up with the little meaningful touches.

"I've got the truck. I'll meet you there."

"Okay."

Before he changed direction, he leaned over and kissed her temple.

The warmth on the spot lasted long after he was gone.

"I bought some potato chips and pop for a treat," Shannyn said in an undertone as Emma spun around the kitchen, still pumped up from her soccer game. "I'm going to run a bath for Em, but if you want you can get those things out."

Jonas leaned casually against the kitchen counter, legs crossed at the ankle. "I can do that."

She paused. "I'll be back in a bit. Emma's going to need a scrubbing."

"I'll be here."

And he would, she realized. For the first time she knew he'd be exactly where he said he'd be. Wondering what had changed was driving her crazy, but Emma had to be tended to first. Normally this was a time of night she enjoyed, but tonight she was impatient to get Emma safely tucked in bed. He was waiting for her.

When they came back downstairs, Jonas was unloading the dishwasher, putting the dishes back on their shelves. Shannyn halted at the bottom of the stairs and stared. He looked so much as though he belonged there. Briefly she got a flash of what life would be like if he were here every day, and it shot straight to her core. She had to be careful. The plain fact was that he was still in the Army, and now that he was nearly recovered, the chance of reassignment was suddenly a possibility. She couldn't allow herself to get used to him when there was a good chance he would be gone again.

Still, the simple action of being here gave her hope that somehow they could compromise, to make it work.

"I smell like bubble gum," Emma announced, letting go of Shannyn's hand and marching over to her father. "Smell my hair."

Dutifully he lifted her up and buried his nose in her curls. "Bubble gum? Smells like blueberries to me."

"Nope. Bubble gum." Her face was a picture of seriousness. "*Pink* bubble gum."

Jonas laughed. "I hope you didn't brush your teeth yet. Your treat's on the table."

Emma scrambled down and ran for her chair and the bowl of chips he'd set out. He followed her and poured her glass half-full of root beer.

He was so good with her, Shannyn realized. For a man who hadn't wanted children, he was a natural. Decisive but fun, willing to play a little. She'd been wrong in keeping Emma from him. When she'd realized she was pregnant, she should have told him somehow. And for that she owed him an apology. A real one, not one out of guilt that came from being caught. And she needed to apologize for depriving him of what should have been his all along—the joy of being Emma's father.

"Penny for your thoughts." He smiled and her heart turned over.

"Later," she replied, her cheeks blooming. It was almost as though she was transported back six years to the man she remembered—the young man filled with optimism and energy. Knowing now what he'd been through, all that he'd faced, how he'd suffered and how he was bouncing back, made him into so much more in her eyes. A dangerous, potent combination of charm and manliness.

She turned away, feigning attention to Emma. Relaxed mood or not, it frightened her to realize how deep her feelings ran for him. She loved him more now than she ever had, she realized. Suddenly her earlier joy and hope faded. She'd had her heart broken once; she was afraid to give him the power to do it again.

Nothing made sense. She wanted him, loved him, admired his parental instincts. Yet she still felt she had to hold back, to protect herself on some level. Fool me once, shame on you. Fool me twice…she didn't want to be that woman.

Emma finished her snack and Jonas took her up to bed, storybook in hand. When he came down several minutes later, Shannyn was just finishing tidying the mess left over from the snack.

Suddenly, now that they were alone, it felt awkward. Shannyn wasn't sure what to say, and Jonas stood in the kitchen looking as if he felt the same way. Saying they needed to talk, and then putting it off for over an hour had put everything off-kilter.

"Would you like a drink?"

"I'd love one. Especially if it means I can sit in the shadows with you and drink it."

Her heart gave a heavy thump as she reached into the fridge for two bottles of beer. The flirtatious response did funny things to her insides and she cautioned herself to remain objective. Seeing him walk across the soccer field had filled her with optimism. But now…now she wasn't so sure. Reality was beginning to settle in and there were a lot of things to tackle. Including her own insecurities.

She twisted off the top and handed him the bottle. "Bumps," she said, and they tilted their bottles so that the bottoms knocked gently.

It was a movement so familiar, yet one long forgotten. Without warning, memory upon memory seemed to be coming back to her about their time together. Trying to isolate how she felt then and how she felt now. It was becoming more difficult as her feelings escalated. They all seemed to blend together, as though it had only been yesterday rather than years.

Outside, the air had cooled, the summer evening breeze fluttering over her skin. Shannyn sat in a chair and leaned back, stretching her legs. She knew he had something on his mind. She forced herself to be patient and wait for him. It would be better that way, if she let him take the lead. She took a deep breath of air softly perfumed by the blooms in her flower bed.

Jonas paused, then turned the opposite chair so that it was at a ninety-degree angle to her and likewise, sat.

After a moment or two of silence, his voice cut through the night sounds of the breeze flickering the leaves and a mourning dove just finishing its song.

"I have a lot to explain to you, Shan. I didn't fully realize it until today, so bear with me okay?"

She nodded. Any trace of flippancy he'd shown inside was totally gone. Now his face was completely earnest.

"I did as you suggested, as you know. I started seeing a therapist after Canada Day. It…it hasn't been easy. Sometimes—" He stopped, swallowed. "Sometimes it's been like living through it all over again. But it was the right thing to do. I'm getting better."

Shannyn encouraged him softly. "I know you are. I can see it. You're less on edge. Relaxed, freer with your smiles." She recalled the chaos of July First, then the few times he'd been in contact since. "I think not seeing you as much made the difference stand out more each time you *were* around. You were more changed each time. More grounded."

"I didn't realize it was noticeable."

"I noticed." She touched his knee gently, then took another drink from her bottle.

The mourning dove's cry faded away. "Today is one year since the accident."

"I know."

His gaze met hers then. "You do?"

She nodded. "I saw the date on your chart." She hadn't forgotten it. It was a day that had changed his life forever. When she'd first read it, she'd had no idea how much. She'd been so absorbed with herself and protecting Emma. She hadn't known how much more there really was.

"Was it difficult? How did you deal?" She'd thought of him often today, wondered how he was coping, wanting to call but unsure of whether or not she should.

"Today I drove to Nova Scotia, to Chris's hometown. And I went to visit him."

Shannyn put down her bottle. "That's a huge step for you." It had obviously been a good choice. If not, he wouldn't be here now.

"I was scared. Facing him…seeing his grave…I didn't know how I'd react. I've been such a loose cannon. But I stopped and bought us each a coffee." He looked up, a shy smile teasing the corners of his mouth. "Sounds stupid, I know, but in basic we had this thing about coffee in the morning. So I took one to him, and I just talked to him. It was good."

Shannyn's eyes misted. She doubted Jonas realized how much strength he was exhibiting right now. Facing the past took courage, and in her eyes, letting himself be vulnerable made him more of a man than any war he'd fought.

She reached over and laid her hand on his thigh. It was nearly healed, the muscle firm and sure beneath her fingers.

"Oh, Jonas, that's wonderful."

"I needed to do it. I'd made him a promise, you see. We always said that if something happened to one of us, the other one would escort the body home. I broke that vow. I didn't come back with him. Hell, I didn't even make his funeral. By the time I was stabilized and conscious, it was all over. Today I apologized for that."

Shannyn smiled. "You do realize that he forgave you long ago. You needed to forgive yourself."

He pulled his leg away from hers. "That's one of the things I'm beginning to see."

"You couldn't have known what would happen, and you couldn't have stopped it." She halted, unsure how much to reveal to him right now. He'd asked for space and she'd said she'd give it, but tonight seemed to be about honesty. Could she be honest with her feelings? Or was it too soon?

"You don't know how thankful I am that you weren't the one killed." She offered a compromise.

"But I came back and complicated everything for you."

"Maybe at first." She smiled sadly. "I was afraid. Fear is a powerful motivator."

Jonas rubbed a hand over his face. "I know. I wrote the book on it. Which brings me to what happened next." He studied his hands, rubbing the fingers together. "Someone else was visiting him, too. Nessa."

"Nessa?"

"His fiancée. He was planning on marrying her after that last deployment. We were only supposed to have another month or so before coming home for a while. The day we hit the mine, he'd told me she'd just bought her dress. I'd never met her, but I met her today."

"How is she?"

Shannyn studied him closely. Jonas smiled a little. In the trees at the edge of the yard, bats flitted in and out as darkness settled over them. The light over the kitchen stove filtered through the patio doors and threw his face in shadow.

"She's amazing. Resilient. And when I saw her today I knew I'd made a huge mistake.

"Even though Chris is gone, she is determined to honor him by living her life and being happy. She cherishes their time together, instead of being bitter and resentful. Nessa is grateful, Shan." His tone was incredulous, reverent. "She's simply grateful that she had the chance to love him. Even though that love was cut short."

He put his bottle down. "And that's where you come in, Shan."

Nerves skittered along her arms. "Me?"

"I owe you an apology. I did what I thought was right all those years ago. I went to become an elite soldier in an uncertain world. I thought that I was right in leaving you behind. I was afraid to have you care for me too much. What would have happened to you if I'd died in action? If I never came home again? Or if I came home crippled and you had to look after me? How could I ask you to waste your life like that? And now I'm telling you that I was wrong. I'm sorry. More sorry than you know that it's too late to take it back."

Shannyn closed her eyes against the pain searing her heart, only to have the tears that had shimmered there escape and trickle down her cheeks. Not *I'm sorry but I'll make things right*. His closing words echoed in her mind— *It's too late*. She'd been right to keep her feelings to herself just now. He saw her as a mistake he couldn't undo. And as happy as she was for him that he was finding his way back, the bitter taste of regret was on her tongue. He'd hurt her then and he was hurting her now.

"You say now that you did what you thought was best for me," she whispered through the pain. "But you never asked me." Her throat ached, raw. "You took away my choice. How could you do that?"

"I thought I was protecting you."

One of his hands rose to touch her cheek, the pad of his thumb caressing her cheekbone. He could be so tender, so caring, and it ripped her apart. She pulled her cheek away from his touch as the hurt spilled out with the truth. "You broke my heart, Jonas. Don't you realize that?"

She opened her eyes. Jonas didn't know that the words were as true tonight as they'd been six years ago. His face was a mixture of regret and surprise.

"No, I didn't. I thought we cared about each other but that you'd get over it. We were young, foolish."

"Foolish or not, I fell in love with you that summer."

Jonas slid forward so that their knees were touching. "So did I."

Shannyn sat up straighter. He'd what? Her heart pounded heavily, her throat convulsing against the tears she kept fighting back. All this time she'd thought that summer had been fun for him, nothing more. He'd loved her? Her head spun. How things could have been different if she'd only known. She would have fought harder, instead of accepting his disappearance from her life. If only he'd said something, all this time might not have been wasted. How stupid they'd been. How much they'd lost.

"But you never said it," she whispered.

"Neither did you."

"I was waiting for you to say it first."

It sounded juvenile now, and made her angry, knowing that perhaps if they'd just been honest back then things might have turned out differently.

"It was a test, then?"

Jonas said the words quietly but there was an edge to his voice that made her look away. Had she been testing him? She'd been young and in love and unsure of everything. She hadn't wanted to beg for his feelings, and perhaps her pride had gotten in the way. Pride and fear had kept her from contacting him once she'd known she was pregnant. Fear that the worst would happen. That he wouldn't love her as she loved him. Fear that he'd come home in a box. Fear that he'd be wounded. In that, she hadn't been wrong. It was small consolation.

"If it was, it wasn't intentional."

Her response sounded flimsy and she bit her lip. Would she have wanted him to choose her over the Army? Is that what she wanted now?

She didn't like the answer that came back.

"We both made mistakes." He was still apologizing, as though he was the only one carrying any responsibility around. "I took the choice away from you, Shannyn. I wasn't honest with my feelings. I wanted to ask you to come with me. But then I thought of all the service men who never came home and I knew I'd hate myself for hurting you. I made my decision based on fear, not on faith. Faith in you, faith in us. I realized that today. I took that choice away and I'm sorry. More sorry than you'll ever know."

His hand squeezed her wrist, warming the skin with a gentle touch before letting go. All these years she'd thought he hadn't cared enough to stay, or to ask her to wait for him. But he had cared. He'd made a mistake, yes. He'd taken the choice away from her. But he'd done it for the right reasons. Not out of concern for himself, but for her. He'd done it out of love. Could she say the same? She knew she couldn't, and it made her own admission sting that much more.

"I'm sorry, too, Jonas. I thought you hadn't loved me at all, so when I found out I was pregnant with Emma I knew I couldn't ask you to come back out of obligation. It would hurt too much to know you didn't love me the way I loved you. So I kept it from you. I denied you your daughter and denied her a father who clearly loves her. And I denied us the chance at a future. You're not the only one with regrets and with apologies." If only he knew.

"It's over now." He sat up a bit, holding her hand between both of his and chafing it. "No more looking back. No more regrets. What's done is done and we go from here."

Where exactly was that, though? Shannyn realized that while Jonas had said that he'd loved her then, he hadn't said that he still did now. There was something between them, certainly. But neither of them had said the word *love* and referred to it in the present tense. Once again she was waiting for him to say it first, too afraid to take the first step. Too afraid that they were repeating the same pattern. Could she bear for him to stay in the service, knowing how quickly their lives could change? Could she risk putting Emma through it, as well as herself? It wasn't just her to consider anymore.

"Where do we go from here?" she asked quietly, withdrawing her hands. "What do *you* see happening between us, Jonas?"

"I don't know." Jonas sighed and rested his elbows on his knees. "I've spent so much time living in the past that I'm not even in the future yet. I'm still taking things one day at a time. I'm going to have some decisions to make soon about where my future lies. I…"

He stopped midsentence, turned his head and looked out over the backyard.

"You what?"

"Tonight I had to tell you the truth about why I left. And for the first time, today I actually started thinking about the future rather than just being in crisis mode, taking things one day at a time. I've been there for so long, it's hard to get out."

His gaze met hers. Even, honest. "I still need time. Time to figure everything out. I'm going away for a few days. To talk to some people. Figure out my options."

Shannyn sat back in her chair, putting some distance between them. She wanted to say, *You've had six years to figure it out,* but knew it would be unfair. He was making progress. It was good he was moving forward. It wasn't up to her to approve of the direction he chose. The longer they talked, the clearer that became.

Perhaps that was why his next words shook her to the core.

"I'm not sure what the future holds, Shannyn. But I am clear on one thing. I never should have left you six years ago."

After all these years, finally hearing the words didn't feel the way she'd expected. It made her deeply mourn the time they'd wasted. Made her resent the choice he'd made. If only he'd stayed. Perhaps they could have worked it out. If he'd just asked her to go with him…

But she imagined hearing that knock on her door in the middle of the night. Imagined what it must have been like for Nessa. She didn't want to be a young woman standing beside a grave.

"You don't seem happy."

His voice, flat and expressionless, reached her and she snapped her head up to meet his gaze.

"It's not that…it's just…why are you telling me this today?"

"It doesn't matter."

She started to panic. He was taking her reaction as rejection, and she desperately needed to understand. "It does matter, Jonas. It matters a great deal." When he made to get out of the chair, she reached out and stopped him with a hand on his arm.

He sat back. "You want to know why today? Because I'm not afraid anymore. I needed to come clean. It's that simple."

Shannyn inhaled, the air trembling on its way to her lungs. "Nothing between us has ever been simple."

"No."

He needed to make a clean break. It was all making sense now. The words hung in the air as the silence grew thick around them. She couldn't bring herself to answer. She couldn't imagine de- lineating all the reasons why they couldn't be together. He'd made a mistake in the past, he'd made that clear. And she forgave him for it. What good would it do to talk about it now? It would change nothing.

Her eyes stung. So much for taking that leap of faith.

Jonas pushed back his chair and stood. His weight was even over both feet, and again Shannyn was reminded of how far he'd come over the past few months with his recovery. Jonas was putting his body and his life back together. She needed to do the same. She couldn't live her life waiting for him to make deci- sions. She'd learned that the hard way, and she and Emma had been okay. Having him around again, she'd started to think of him as part of their lives. Now she realized she had to stand on her own two feet again.

"Come here," he murmured in the dark.

She went to him, the evening breeze chilling her, raising goose bumps on her flesh. He pulled her lightly into his arms, resting his temple against her hair.

"You've given me strength, Shannyn Smith. You've given me the strength and the courage to get through this. Don't you think I'll ever forget that. I owe you everything."

She sighed, drank in his scent one last time. Imprinted on her heart every sensation of his body against hers. Then she pushed away.

"I'm happy for you."

Shannyn was surprised at how strong she sounded. She instantly missed the warmth of his arms around her. But as much as she knew she loved him, she also knew what he was saying. He was still who he was…*what* he was. He hadn't made promises, or proclaimed any feelings. The very strength that she'd wished for him was now driving him away, and she couldn't find the will to voice her feelings. She was too afraid. Afraid of losing him. Afraid of growing farther apart during his absences rather than closer together. Afraid that despite their renewed relationship, she'd always be the one that loved more. That hurt more.

She reached up and ran her fingers over his shoulders, imagining him in his uniform. She smiled sadly. "You are still a soldier. And now a healthy one. I don't doubt for a minute that this job posting will end and you'll be off on some new adventure. It's who you are, Jonas."

"You're still scared."

"Of course I am. I don't think I could survive losing you again. It's good that it's stopping here."

Everything in her wanted him to fight now. Fight for her like he hadn't six years earlier. Instead he remained silent and what little hope she'd held on to died a quiet death.

"You think my life is too what, transient? Dangerous and uncertain?"

"Something like that."

He wasn't fighting, then. It was over. Really over. It was the ending perhaps they'd never had, but there was no relief in it. All Shannyn felt was cold resignation at the way things had turned out.

She didn't want him to leave but understood now that it was exactly what he was doing. He had made her fall in love with him again, and now he was walking away. Just like before.

When he pulled away, his hand on the railing of the deck, she didn't stop him.

"We covered a lot of ground this evening," he acknowledged. "Maybe it's better to let the dust settle. Then we can meet and talk about where we go from here. We need to talk about Emma. We need to stay consistent for her, no matter what."

"That will be fine." It sounded forced and she knew it.

"I'm not sure when I'll be back. But I'll call you," he said softly. "Give Emma a kiss for me."

"I will," she replied, trying to hold back the tears that suddenly threatened. They were done. Reduced to talking about visitation schedules and what was best for their daughter. Knowing that every time she saw him she'd die a little more inside from loving him so hopelessly.

He hopped off the porch and lifted his hand in a wave before skirting around the house. Moments later his truck started and she heard his tires on the gravel of the drive.

Worn-out and overwhelmed, she sat back down on the chair, letting the sobs finally come. And tried to put together the pieces of what had just happened.

*You've given me the strength and the courage to get through this. Don't you think I'll ever forget that.*

She'd wanted him better, had wanted him to stop suffering, had wanted to help him through it. She just hadn't thought the cost to herself would be so high.

# CHAPTER FOURTEEN

SHANNYN looked at the phone for the umpteenth time that afternoon. Each time it rang and Melanie answered it, her heart skipped a beat. Monday was the same, as was yesterday. Patients came and went; she did spreadsheets and payroll.

There was no reason for her to look for his call, but he was never far from her mind.

He'd been up-front about telling her that he was going away to discuss future options. Who knew what he'd be doing, or where. She remembered the gleam in his eyes as he'd spoken to Cpl. Benner outside the coffee shop. There's nothing he'd love more than to be back with the men of his unit. She knew that.

She should have known things would only grow more complicated. Emma had asked about him on Sunday, and again yesterday. Shannyn had no answers for her. He'd said they needed to talk about Emma, but now he wasn't making himself available. It was what she'd always feared. Shannyn was a grown-up and could deal somehow. But a child didn't understand why Daddy was suddenly *just gone*. Finally, last night, she'd broken down and tried calling his apartment, but there'd been no answer.

She played with a pen sitting on her desk, clicking the tip over and over. Jonas had admitted his mistake of years past. As hard as she tried, she couldn't forget that, even though she had forgiven him for it. Maybe he'd made a mistake leaving her, but the truth of the matter was if he'd loved her so very much, it wouldn't have mattered. He'd have asked her to go with him. No doubt. She realized now she probably *had* been testing him. And she'd punished him by keeping Emma from him.

She ran a hand through her hair. She loved him; she wouldn't lie to herself and attempt to deny it. But loving someone and making it work were two very different things. Now there was Emma in the middle, ensuring he'd always be linked to her somehow. She set her lips and went to the stacks to take out his chart. They needed to talk regardless. She wouldn't let Emma be pushed aside the way she'd been.

With a fortifying breath, she picked up the receiver of her phone and dialed the work number from his file.

When she asked for him, the polite woman on the other end apologized. "I'm sorry, ma'am, he's on base in Petawawa."

On base? Being out of town explained why he hadn't called, and she relaxed. "Do you know when he'll be back?"

The line was silent as the woman hesitated for a moment. "That will depend ma'am, on if he starts his new posting."

Shannyn sat down in her chair, suddenly numb. *New posting?* Jonas was going to a new posting? And he hadn't told her, or Emma? When had he decided? After they'd talked? Or had he known that night when he'd shown up at the soccer game?

Emma. Oh, no. Her heart sank to her toes. Shannyn had her own disappointments, but Emma was different. She was too small to understand a father coming and going, always in and out of her life. Realizing she still loved him had provoked all the old fears. Shannyn had known in the beginning that no one in the military stayed in one place for long. Over the past few weeks she'd conveniently forgotten it. How could she ever tell Emma that her dad had been killed in action? She'd almost wanted him to retain some of his injury so returning to active duty wouldn't be an option. It was purely selfish, she knew. And she truly was glad for him that his leg was healed and he felt whole again. Oh, what a mess she was in.

"Ma'am? Do you want to leave a message?"

"No," Shannyn muttered hoarsely. "No, thank you."

She hung up the phone heavily. Suddenly things he'd said became clear. Thanking her for being strong for him. Saying he'd never forget it. No more looking back and no regrets. She'd felt it was goodbye and it looked like her intuition had been right on the money. His file still lay on her desk. She hadn't given him a reason to stay. She had no one to blame but herself.

Nausea rolled through her stomach. She'd done it again. She'd lost her heart to him only to have him leave her without asking her opinion. He'd made decisions already and left her in the dark. Just like then, he'd charted out a life for himself and hadn't asked for her input. Only now there wasn't just her. There was Emma who was going to get hurt.

She let the cold anger roll in, and stacked the items on the top of her desk with terrifying precision. Anger was easier to deal with than the hurt. At least last time she'd known where he was going. It had always been a given. She'd just hoped he would ask her to go along, or leave her with some sort of assurance of keeping their relationship going. This time he was making changes and not even keeping her in the loop. After the way he'd seemingly bonded with Emma, it was hard to believe he'd do something like this without considering their daughter. She thought he'd changed.

She took his chart and shoved it back onto the shelf. She deserved better. Emma deserved better. The way he'd held her, the way he'd won Emma's heart told her he owed them more.

She made it through the remainder of the afternoon simply

by going into automatic pilot. She picked up Emma at the sitter's, chatted mindlessly with her about painting and grape Popsicles, all the while stewing about how she'd ended up in this place again. Vulnerable to him. Waiting for him. Waiting for a man who wasn't coming.

Shannyn took the key out of the ignition with a sigh. She felt used. Now that he was better physically, and making great strides emotionally, she felt that she was no longer needed. She'd been there while he'd been struggling, but now that he was moving on with his life, she was forgettable. The woman who had helped him through his *rough time.* Someone he'd once loved.

She'd promised herself she'd never let herself be vulnerable again, but here she was. Left behind. Again.

Emma bounced into the house ahead of her mother. "What's for dinner?" She skidded to a stop in the kitchen, her day care backpack dropping to the floor. Shannyn bit back her irritation; it wasn't Emma's fault she was in such a tumult.

"I don't know."

"Can we have mac and cheese? Can we?"

Shannyn's eyes caught the red blinking light of the answering machine. Holding up a finger to silence Emma for a moment, she hit the button.

The first message was from Patty, saying that she was taking Lisa to the diner around six and asking if Emma would like to go along.

"Yes, yes, yes!" Emma called out, dragging her backpack through the kitchen to the table. "The diner beats macaroni and cheese!" She started pulling things out of her pack.

The second message was from Jonas.

"Shan, it's me. I need to see you. I know it's short notice, but could you come by tonight? Anytime after five-thirty is great."

It was ridiculous, how she was affected by the mere sound of him on an answering machine. Even knowing what she did now, the husky timbre of his voice reached inside of her. She steeled herself. Likely he was going to break the news to her tonight. A new posting meant moving on. After what she'd said, she knew it meant moving on without her.

"Can I come see Daddy, too?"

Shannyn hated to say no but this was one time she knew she and Jonas would be better off alone. "I thought you were going to the diner."

"Oh, yeah."

"Daddy and I need to discuss some grown-up things anyway. You'd be bored." Shannyn paused, wanting to be encouraging to Emma but not giving her false guarantees that she couldn't deliver. "I'll talk to him, though, and see when he plans on visiting again, okay?"

Emma nodded, not too upset, apparently. Shannyn exhaled slowly. If he *were* going away, she'd make sure he spent time with Emma before he went. That was nonnegotiable.

She called Patty and accepted the invitation, then asked if Emma could stay there until she got back from an errand. But that left her with the problem of time on her hands and trying to keep occupied until Emma was picked up. She sorted the laundry and put a load in the washer, vacuumed the living room. Sat with Emma and read a few stories. When six finally arrived, she heaved a great sigh of relief.

Once Emma was gone Shannyn considered revamping her appearance. She changed into a pretty skirt and blouse, then looked in the mirror and frowned. This was ridiculous. She was bracing herself for a breakup, which was funny because they weren't really together in the first place. It was silly to dress up and look extraspecial. She changed out of the skirt and slid back into her comfy jeans and T-shirt. Again she met her own gaze in the mirror. If he were truly going to destroy her world, she was at least going to be in comfortable clothes.

Tucking her hair behind her ears one last time, she took her purse, got in her car, and drove toward the end.

Jonas answered the buzzer, a smile of relief breaking out on his face. He smoothed his hands down his shirt, making sure it was tucked neatly into his waistband. He hadn't even changed out of the dress uniform he'd worn today when he'd met the Minister of Defence. He'd removed his tie and red beret, but that was it. Somehow, tonight required more than jeans and a ratty T-shirt.

When five-thirty had passed, he'd started to worry. Had considered calling again but decided against it. Perhaps she was running late or couldn't get a sitter for Emma. Finally he'd given in and dialled the phone again.

The door buzzed when he was hearing the third ring, and he hung up.

Tonight was going to change everything.

He held the door open for her, surprised when she breezed past him coolly. He frowned. Her dander was up about something, although he couldn't imagine what.

"Thank you for coming," he started, his head turning to follow her as she sailed through the small foyer. There was so much he had to say. To explain.

"So, when do you start?"

"I beg your pardon?" His steps halted behind her.

Shannyn zipped straight through to the living room, planting her hands on her hips. After a momentary lapse, he followed her, confused. What was she talking about? And why in the world was she acting as if he was the villain? Her eyes met his, full of a challenge he didn't understand.

"Your new job? When do you start? Where is it this time?"

Staccato words, so harsh. She raised one eyebrow at him, her lips set in a firm, unpleasant line. All his well-thought-out speeches evaporated. How could she possibly know? He'd only been offered the position this morning, and he'd caught the first hop back to Gagetown. He'd been home all of three hours.

"Shannyn, I can explain. All of it." He folded his hands behind his back, trying to remain rational and not take the bait for an all-out argument. Even if her aggressive stance did try his temper.

"Oh, there's no need. I heard all about it today. Petawawa, right? Is that where you're going next? Or back with the Princess Pats in Edmonton? Where are you *needed* this time?"

"Why are you acting like this? You're so angry!" He stepped further into the room, shoving his hands into the pockets of his trousers. If she'd only give him a chance to explain. Instead she was treating him as though he'd done something unforgivable. "You sent me away, remember?"

Damn. He'd told himself she wouldn't draw him into an argument, and here he was, rising to the bait.

She folded her arms with defiance. "Maybe I'm angry because I finally trusted you. I trusted you to be honest, Jonas. If not for me, for Emma. And now I find out from someone else that you're taking a new job." She held up her hand when he started to protest. "No, don't bother. I know a new job means a new posting and a new base. I've enough experience with the Army to know *that* much. This is exactly why I didn't tell you about Emma in the first place, Jonas. Because I didn't want her to know—to love— a father who was only in her life when his schedule permitted."

"Only Emma?" He smiled a little. She was covering her misgivings with blame. He took it as a good sign. Their parting last week had been surprisingly cold. But now the thought of him going away had her panicking. "Or are you afraid I'll only let *you* in my life when I can pencil you in?"

"That's ridiculous. And it doesn't matter. You're obviously leaving again."

"You're wrong." His voice was firm but sure. He could see what was happening. He recognized the fear, knew it was much more promising than not caring at all. He knew she was remembering how he'd left her before, and it kept him from getting too angry with her. If she would only listen to him, she'd understand everything.

"Oh, please. Don't insult me," she retorted.

"Don't insult *me*, Shannyn." He kept his voice even. "I don't know what you think you know, but perhaps you'd be interested in hearing the actual truth."

Her brazen sneer faltered just a little.

"This isn't about Emma. Not really. It's about you, and you being afraid that I'll leave you again."

Her mouth dropped open.

"You think I don't get it? After we talked last week? I know now how I hurt you the last time. I don't blame you for being scared. You don't want to go through it again. You don't want to go through what Nessa has gone through. And believe me, I've no desire to put you through it."

"Why would you, when you clearly said goodbye?"

"Is that what you think?"

"Isn't it true?"

He smiled a little. She was more afraid than he'd thought. He thought back to their conversation. He hadn't meant it as goodbye at all. He'd thought they'd been finding their feet. Setting the groundwork upon which to build something great.

And she thought he'd been preparing to leave for good.

He could see the vulnerability through her aggressive stance, and softened his voice, trying to draw her in, make her understand.

He tilted her chin, lifting it so that his eyes burned into hers. "Do. You. Love. Me. It's that simple, Shan."

"Nothing is ever that simple. You know that."

"I know I love you. Do you love me back?"

Tears burned the backs of her eyes. He was standing here saying it after all, and she hated how much she wanted to hope. To believe. Damn him. Damn him for making her feel so much all over again.

"Please," he murmured. Her eyelids fluttered closed as he dropped tiny kisses on them, the light touch making her sway. "Please tell me the truth."

She nodded, her forehead brushing his cheek as the answer came out in a strangled whisper— "Yes."

"Yes, you love me?"

She blinked, and two tears ran silently over her cheeks. "Yes, I love you."

Instead of the heated kiss of earlier, he drew her tenderly into his arms, resting his chin against her hair.

"Think about this for a moment. Would I have told you I loved you if I were going to give up on us?"

"I don't know." The vigor deflated out of her argument, the vulnerability creeping closer to the surface. She pulled out of his arms and away, where she could think clearly. "I…I'm not sure of anything where you're concerned."

"And that scares you." He took a step closer.

Shannyn inhaled, trying to stop the shaking, trying to keep up the bravado. He was being so steady. Looking so tall and heroic and handsome in his uniform.

She'd thought that just laying it all on the table would be less painful, like ripping off a bandage. She'd come in here with both barrels blazing, taking the offensive to cover her concerns and hurt. Full of resolve, knowing it was over between them. But, damn him, he'd seen right through it. She'd felt strong in her righteous indignation. Now here he was telling her she was wrong. Recognizing she was scared. And, oh, she was so sick of living in fear. With his words, she'd gone from being on the offensive to being left with very little defense.

"Shan," he continued. Another step. "Tell me what scares you. Trust me with it. I trusted you."

"This is different," she murmured. "Because *you* scare me. I'm scared to love you."

Jonas came all the way to where she was standing. Close enough it would only take a breath and she would feel him against her. Only inches separated them. But still he did not touch her.

"Faith, not fear," he murmured. If only he'd realized it sooner. "I hurt you so badly the first time. I know that now. And because of it you doubt me."

"Maybe I need a reason not to."

He lifted her chin with a finger, touching her skin there but nowhere else. "Then how's this for starters. I loved you then. I love you more now. Even more today than I did last week. And I want to spend the rest of my life proving it."

Tears sprung into her eyes and she blinked them away. She couldn't breathe.

She couldn't let herself be placated so easily, not when the simple words did splendid things to her insides.

"Then why didn't you tell me what you were doing?" She challenged him, pulling her chin away from his caress. "A phone call, or even an e-mail to let me know your plans. Instead you walked away. For all I knew it was for good."

He smiled. "I can see that you think that, and I'm sorry. It's not what I intended. I wanted to be honest with you about the past so we could put it behind us. I didn't mean to give you the impression that I was putting *us* behind *me*. I told you I was exploring some options, remember? But nothing was definite, so I didn't want to tell you prematurely and get your hopes up. I had meetings with some men in Ontario, it's true. About my future."

There were still too many blanks to fill in. "What sorts of options?" The earlier thought of active duty leaped to front and center. The thought of him going back out in the field, to the front line of danger…the threat of losing him always present…she couldn't lie; she wished he'd do something other than rejoin his unit. Something safer.

"There's something I have to know first."

"What?"

They stood only inches apart, a standoff. Yet Shannyn felt inexorably tied to him. Like there was a cord binding them together, even when they were coming from different places.

"If my life were more settled, would you give us a chance?"

All the air seemed to squeeze out of her chest. "How can you ask that, without giving me details?"

"It's easy. Don't make it more complicated than it is. Forget my job. Forget the past. Forget Emma. Ask yourself if you are willing to take the risk now. If you trust me to do the right thing."

His eyes softened, her gaze was drawn to his full lips as he formed the words.

How could she do it? Walk blindly into a life of uncertainty? Live with the danger, knowing he could be taken away from her at any time?

She'd only wanted him to ask her the last time, but it was much more than that. Loving him meant accepting the possibility of being hurt.

"Faith, not fear." He whispered the gentle reminder.

She watched his mouth form the words. It didn't matter. She was hurting right now. And he was standing before her, the strongest man she'd ever known, asking her to share his life. Without guarantees.

She knew the answer as it shot out of her heart.

"Yes." The words choked out on a near sob. "I need you, Jonas. It's what scares me more than anything."

Letting the words out, confessing her feelings and her fears, felt like complete surrender, and for a moment she reveled in the freedom of it. Her eyes slid closed as he came closer, dropping his lips to touch hers gently.

"That's really good news," he murmured against her lips. "Because I thought I was alone in that particular area."

Her lips followed his, eager to taste more, now that they'd said the words. "Loving you comes naturally. Dealing with it is the hard part."

She was suddenly reminded of his new posting and she drew back. "But you're leaving, aren't you? Are you going back into active duty? Being stationed at another base?" Dread at losing him, anyway, curled darkly through her.

"If I were transferred, would you come with me? You and Emma?"

This, then, was the question he'd never asked the first time, and even though she couldn't help the thread of anxiety at the thought of leaving her home and job behind, she knew this time she couldn't back away.

"Yes. Yes, Jonas, I would come with you this time."

"Why?"

She looked up at him. Over the time she'd known him, he'd been three men. The first was the carefree, indestructible warrior. The second a hard, uncompromising man broken by the things he'd seen and done. The third, though, the third was a mixture of those two men. A man so much stronger than the two parts that made him who he was. In his eyes she saw not only shades of his youth but a wisdom and gravity that only experience could bring. A man who felt deeply, loved his job, loved his daughter. Loved her. How could she ever let that get away? How could she give up the chance to love him? Maybe he would be back in the line of fire. But she knew that if she passed up the chance to try, she'd regret it always, and she told him so.

"Because I love you. Because I'm tired of being scared, too. I let you leave before because I thought you didn't love me. I didn't tell you about Emma because I was afraid you'd be with us for the wrong reasons and so I built a wall around my heart, told myself I was doing the right thing. I came here tonight, ready to tear into you because I was afraid to love you more than you loved me. But I do love you, I always have and being *without* you now is more terrifying than any of those things."

His hand cupped the back of her neck, roughly pulling her close and cradling her head against his chest. His pulse thudded against her temple, steady and strong. She felt him swallow, press a kiss against her hair.

"I promise I won't give you reason to regret it. I know the risk you're taking, and I love you more for it. But I don't have to leave, Shan."

She pulled out of his arms. "You don't? But what about Petawawa? The new posting?"

His teeth flashed as he smiled. "I did go to Petawawa. And I did have meetings, and I've been offered a position. But I haven't accepted it yet."

"Why not?"

"Because I needed to talk it over with you first. It wouldn't be fair to make that sort of decision without finding out how you and Emma feel about it."

Suddenly the tears came, great consuming ones that surprised her as much as they surprised Jonas. She hadn't even realized she'd been testing him again or that this had been part of it, but his consulting her meant more than he could ever know.

"Shhh," he murmured, cupping her face and wiping away tears. "You haven't even heard what it is yet."

A bubble of laughter rose up through the sobs. "That's not why." She pressed a hand to her chest and regained control. "How can I tell you what I think about it if you don't tell me what it is?"

He grinned. "You'll be pleased to know the job is right here. At Base Gagetown."

"No active duty?"

He gripped her arms. "Is that what you thought?"

She nodded, flooded with relief that he wasn't going to be back in the field after all.

"No, baby, no active duty. An opportunity came up. One so good I didn't want to jinx it by saying anything prematurely. You and Emma…I didn't want to uproot you from the lives you've worked so hard to build. I can see how you've created a real home for her. I want to be a part of that, Shan, not take her away from it."

She blinked slowly. He was doing a fine job of building his case. Right now she was spellbound, hanging on his every word with breathless anticipation.

"I was offered a contract through the SAS to train Special Forces. Everything's being spearheaded out of Petawawa, but the majority of training will be at the Combat Arms Center here. Included in that is a chance to be a liaison with the government for antiterrorism."

"Oh, Jonas. You must be so proud. Of course you must take it."

"It's a choice assignment. I couldn't ask for better. I couldn't answer, though, until I knew what you wanted. All I knew is that it could keep me where I belong—with you and Emma. If…"

"If…"

She held her breath.

He reached into his trousers and pulled out a ring, the platinum and single diamond catching the dying sunbeams in the fading light. "I should have done this years ago, but better late than never." He gripped her left hand in his strong right one. "If you'll marry me. Give me a chance to be the husband and father you both deserve. Let us build a family together." His eyes twinkled at her. "Maybe even a bigger family."

She put the fingers of her right hand over her lips, unsure of whether to laugh or cry. She'd come here tonight prepared for a standoff, not a proposal. Not the answer to all her hopes and dreams. And she'd come in her ratty jeans, she thought. A spurt of laughter crept up and out her lips.

"You haven't said yes yet," he reminded her.

"It's about time I made that leap of faith, don't you think?" Her fingers trembled but her smile was wide. "Put it on, Jonas. Put on the ring and make us a family."

He slid the ring over her knuckle, the diamond winking as she wiggled her fingers.

She lifted both her hands to cup his face.

"I love you. No matter what, you'll always be a hero to me. You just remember that, Sgt. Kirkpatrick."

"I'm not a hero, Shan. I'm just a man. A man who loves you. Always have, always will."

He sealed the covenant with a kiss. "Hey, Shan?"

"Hmmm?"

"Let's go tell Emma."

Sharing conspiratorial smiles, she tugged him by the hand to the door.

"I think we're about to make her day," Shannyn said, laughing.

## The Taken

Tierney Doyle is used to being criticized for
her psychic abilities, yet the tough-as-nails—
and drop-dead-gorgeous—detective has no doubt
about what she has uncovered in the case of a
string of unsolved murders. And Tierney is slowly
discovering that working so close to her partner,
detective Wade Callahan, could be lethal.

Look for

# *Danger Signals*

# by Kathleen Creighton

*Available in April wherever books are sold.*

# REQUEST YOUR FREE BOOKS!
## 2 FREE NOVELS PLUS 2
## FREE GIFTS!

### HARLEQUIN ROMANCE®

## From the Heart, For the Heart

**YES!** Please send me 2 FREE Harlequin Romance® novels and my 2 FREE gifts. After receiving them, if I don't wish to receive any more books, I can return the shipping statement marked "cancel." If I don't cancel, I will receive 4 brand-new novels every month and be billed just $3.57 per book in the U.S., or $4.05 per book in Canada, plus 25¢ shipping and handling per book and applicable taxes, if any*. That's a savings of over 15% off the cover price! I understand that accepting the 2 free books and gifts places me under no obligation to buy anything. I can always return a shipment and cancel at any time. Even if I never buy another book from Harlequin, the two free books and gifts are mine to keep forever.                    114 HDN EEV7  314 HDN EEWK

Name                                (PLEASE PRINT)

Address                                                                   Apt.

City                          State/Prov.                    Zip/Postal Code

Signature (if under 18, a parent or guardian must sign)

Mail to the **Harlequin Reader Service®:**
**IN U.S.A.:** P.O. Box 1867, Buffalo, NY 14240-1867
**IN CANADA:** P.O. Box 609, Fort Erie, Ontario L2A 5X3

Not valid to current Harlequin Romance subscribers.

### Want to try two free books from another line?
### Call 1-800-873-8635 or visit www.morefreebooks.com.

* Terms and prices subject to change without notice. NY residents add applicable sales tax. Canadian residents will be charged applicable provincial taxes and GST. This offer is limited to one order per household. All orders subject to approval. Credit or debit balances in a customer's account(s) may be offset by any other outstanding balance owed by or to the customer. Please allow 4 to 6 weeks for delivery.

**Your Privacy:** Harlequin is committed to protecting your privacy. Our Privacy Policy is available online at www.eHarlequin.com or upon request from the Reader Service. From time to time we make our lists of customers available to reputable firms who may have a product or service of interest to you. If you would prefer we not share your name and address, please check here. ☐

HR07

# Silhouette®

# SPECIAL EDITION™

## Introducing a brand-new miniseries

# Men of Mercy Medical

Gabe Thorne moved to Las Vegas to open a new branch of his booming construction business—and escape from a recent tragedy. But when his teenage sister showed up pregnant on his doorstep, he really had his hands full. Luckily, in turning to Dr. Rebecca Hamilton for the medical care his sister needed, he found a cure for himself....

## Starting with

# THE MILLIONAIRE AND THE M.D.

## by *TERESA SOUTHWICK,*

*available in April wherever books are sold.*

# Coming Next Month

Spring is in the air this month with brides, babies and single dads, and the start of two new can't-miss series: *The Wedding Planners* and *A Bride for All Seasons.*

### #4015 WEDDING BELLS AT WANDERING CREEK RANCH
Patricia Thayer
*Western Weddings*

Dark, brooding detective Jack allows no one to get close—until he takes on stunning Willow's case. His head tells him to run a mile, but will he listen to his heart instead?

### #4016 THE BRIDE'S BABY  Liz Fielding
*A Bride for All Seasons*

Events manager Sylvie Smith has been roped into pretending to be a bride for a wedding fair—but she's five months pregnant, and the father doesn't know yet! Then she comes face-to-face with him...and his eyes are firmly fixed on her bump.

### #4017 SWEETHEART LOST AND FOUND  Shirley Jump
*The Wedding Planners*

The first book of the sparkling series in which six women who plan perfect weddings find their own happy endings. Florist Callie made a mistake years ago and let a good man go. Now she keeps her heart safe. But the good man is back, and Callie might just get a second chance!

### #4018 EXPECTING A MIRACLE  Jackie Braun
*Baby on Board*

Pregnant and alone, Lauren moves to the perfect place for her soon-to-be family of two. Then she's blindsided by her anything-but-maternal attraction to her sexy new landlord, Gavin!

### #4019 THE SINGLE DAD'S PATCHWORK FAMILY  Claire Baxter

Being a single parent is hard, especially when there's been heartache in the past. Chase had planned to raise his daughter alone. But then he meets single mum Regan, and the pieces start falling together again.

### #4020 THE LONER'S GUARDED HEART  Michelle Douglas
*Heart to Heart*

Josie's longed-for holiday is in a cabin in an isolated Australian idyll. Her only neighbor for miles is the gorgeous but taciturn Kent Black, who has cut himself off from the world. And Josie can't help but be intrigued....

HRCNM0308